High Fences

Julie White

Julie White

sononis   WINLAW, BRITISH COLUMBIA
PRESS

Copyright © 2007 by Julie White
Cover artwork copyright © 2007 by Joan Larson

Library and Archives Canada Cataloguing in Publication

White, Julie, 1958-
    High fences / Julie White.

ISBN 978-1-55039-163-3

    1 Ponies—Juvenile fiction. I. Title.

PS8645.H58H53 2007   jC813'.6   C2007-905049-2

Sono Nis Press most gratefully acknowledges support for our publishing program
provided by the Government of Canada through the Book Publishing Industry
Development Program (BPIDP) and the Canada Council for the Arts, and by the
Province of British Columbia through the British Columbia Arts Council and the
Book Publishing Tax Credit, Ministry of Provincial Revenue.

Cover and chapter illustration (detail of cover) by Joan Larson
Edited by Laura Peetoom
Copy edited by Dawn Loewen

Published by
Sono Nis Press
Box 160
Winlaw, BC V0G 2J0
1-800-370-5228

books@sononis.com
www.sononis.com

Distributed in the U.S. by
Orca Book Publishers
Box 468
Custer, WA 98240-0468
1-800-210-5277

Printed and bound in Canada by Houghton Boston.

Printed on acid-free paper that is forest friendly
(100% post-consumer recycled paper) and
has been processed chlorine free.

The Canada Council | Le Conseil des Arts
for the Arts | du Canada

To Denim—my good friend and partner
in many adventures

1

Galloping through the corner to the final fence, Robin slipped on a patch of loose sand and nearly fell to his knees.

Faye grabbed for his mane. Her right boot lost the stirrup and she hung over the pony's shoulder. She heaved herself back into the saddle as Robin scrambled to stay upright. His hooves found firm ground, and with a mighty lurch he managed to regain his balance.

They were three strides from the jump. Robin raised his head, coiling his hindquarters under him. The reins flapped uselessly against his neck. There wasn't time for Faye to gather them up; the jump was a stride away.

She fixed her eyes on the far side of the oxer, ignoring the empty stirrup iron bashing against her foot.

Robin sprang into the air half a stride too soon, well back from the fence. Faye threw herself onto his broad neck. They were in the air, arching over the massive oxer, every muscle and tendon in the pony's body straining to clear the width of the jump. Faye buried her face in the black mane, certain Robin wasn't going to make it. She grabbed tight with her legs and prepared for the moment when his legs tangled with the jump's rails, tumbling him to the earth like a wounded bird.

A gentle tremor shook up through her legs into her body. Faye pushed back off Robin's neck as they landed, somehow right side up and on stride. She snatched up the reins and steered the pony through the finish line.

She eased him up slowly in a big circle. "You wonderful, wonderful pony!" she cried, patting his damp neck. She couldn't help herself; she threw her arms around his neck and hugged him.

"Good riding, Faye!" someone called as they walked out the gate.

She shook her head. Robin's bravery had saved them, not her riding. Hadn't the spectators seen that?

Outside the ring Lucy took Robin by the reins, her forehead crumpled under the brim of her canvas camp hat.

"Wasn't he amazing?" said Faye. She kicked her feet free of the stirrups and slid down to hug her pony again.

Her grandmother's frown deepened as she ran the stirrup irons up the leathers. "He was darned honest! You were too fast coming around that corner. Any other pony would have just dumped you in front of that fence." Lucy smoothed Robin's heavy black forelock to one side and ran her hand down his long white blaze.

Faye's elation evaporated as swiftly as the sweat on her forehead. "He slipped and I lost my reins."

"And your stirrups, too. How many times have I told

you to keep your heels down?"

At least twice a day since we came to live with you, Faye answered silently. She started to do the math: she was twelve, nearly thirteen, and they'd lived at Hillcroft Farm since she was six...

"Your hair's coming loose," said Lucy, breaking into Faye's plodding calculations. She stuffed a springy red curl under Faye's black helmet. "Where's your hairnet?"

Faye shrugged. "I don't know." She took Robin's reins from Lucy. "I'll cool him out."

Robin was hardly puffing but she wanted to get away. Later she'd listen to her grandmother's stride-by-stride critique of the round and go over ways to improve her performance. Right now she just wanted to be alone with her pony and savour the heady, up-in-the-clouds euphoria of that last magnificent jump.

She unbuttoned the collar of her riding shirt. Under her dark blue jacket, her back was sticky with sweat. She tugged off her cotton gloves, her fingers stained by the black dye. Despite the scorching July heat, Lucy had insisted Faye wear complete riding attire in the championship class.

A loud clunk rang out from the ring as a rail fell. Faye looked over just in time to see a rangy grey horse put on the brakes and refuse the last jump.

"Thank you, Robin, for not doing that," she whispered. "I know I didn't give you much help."

Robin bunted her with his head, too excited to stand around talking.

She led him along the row of stables across from the ring. The bruised arch of her foot throbbed with every step. Faye hardly noticed; her mind was too busy replaying her thrilling ride. At the wash rack she turned on the hose and let Robin have a few slurps. By the time they turned around and made it back to the ring, the class was over.

"How'd it go?" she asked Lucy.

"Tough jump-off. Not too many clears. You should be close to the top." Lucy plucked a rag from the back pocket of her jeans and rubbed away the dried sweat on the pony's neck.

A giddy happiness bubbled up in Faye. Robin was just a pony, smaller than the other competitors, but he was one of the fastest, cleanest jumpers in the class. Certainly the bravest—and he was hers. She pressed her face into his salty neck and sighed.

The placings were awarded from the lowest up. Faye fidgeted as the announcer reached third without calling her and Robin. She held her breath, waiting for second place. Not them again.

Okay, it's just another horse show, she told herself. *Sometimes you win, sometimes you don't. But if only I hadn't messed up that last fence—*

"And in first place: Hillcroft Red Robin ridden by Faye March. Congratulations to our Junior Jumper Champion!"

Lucy tugged the irons down. "Faye, wake up. Come on, girl, you won." She did up Faye's collar, then boosted her into the saddle. "Don't worry about gloves," she added as Faye struggled to pull them on her sweaty hands. "Just get in there!"

Robin pranced into the ring, neck curved and tail high. He snorted and spun away as the presenter approached him with a huge red rosette and a silver trophy. Faye straightened him out.

"I know this is nothing new to *him*," the presenter said, hooking the ribbon onto Robin's bridle. He patted Robin's muscled chest. "You're showing off, aren't you?"

He passed the silver trophy to Faye. "Well done, young lady. You and your pony make an impressive team."

"Thanks," Faye answered proudly, tucking the trophy into the crook of her arm while Robin danced on the spot.

The show photographer snapped their picture. Music blared over the loudspeaker. Robin tossed his head and plunged into a canter. Faye urged him to the front of the other ribbon winners, leading the victory gallop around the ring while the spectators clapped and cheered. The lower-placed riders guided their mounts out the gate after a single round but Faye let Robin continue until they were the only pair left in the ring. She reined him to a walk and went out.

Lucy's cheeks were furrowed with smile lines. She fed Robin a bit of carrot. "Good job, boy. You, too, Faye. Now take him back to the horse trailer and untack him. I'll be right along."

"Sure she will," Faye said to Robin. Lucy's more than

fifty years in the horse business meant the showgrounds were packed with people who knew her and would expect her to stop and chat.

Cradling the trophy in her arm, Faye steered Robin so he was walking in the shade of the shedrow. With Lucy gone, she slouched in the saddle and let the pony amble along on a long rein. The enormous ribbon fluttered from his bridle, proclaiming their victory to all.

"It's just not fair!" A girl's voice came from inside one of the stalls. "That Faye March always wins."

"That's because she's got Hillcroft Red Robin. I could beat her if I had a pony like that," grumbled another voice next door. The occupant came out of the stall and saw Faye and Robin going past. Red-faced, she darted inside her friend's stall.

Faye recognized the girl but couldn't remember her name. She was terrible about keeping track of human names and faces.

She shrugged off the spiteful remarks. "No sense in letting them spoil our win, right, Robin?"

Just the same, she wished Kirsty, her best friend— her only human friend—was there to share in the glory, instead of back at the farm helping Faye's older brother, Riley, with the chores.

Back at the horse trailer, Faye set the trophy in the bed of the truck box and gratefully shed her riding jacket. She haltered the pony and unbuckled his tack. She sponged him off, making sure not a speck of dried sweat remained on his burnished russet hide. Indigo blue highlights gleamed in the damp hair as she slicked away the excess water with a sweat scraper. She finger-combed his black tail so the sand fell out of the coarse hair and examined his joints and tendons closely for signs of strain. By that time, Lucy had finally made it to the horse trailer.

"This fellow's got legs of iron," she remarked, crouching down to run her fingers over the pony's lower legs. She stood up, her old knees cracking.

Robin sipped water from the bucket Faye held up to him and picked at his hay net.

Lucy wet her fingers in the bucket and dribbled them under the collar of her plaid cotton shirt. "Whew, it's a warm one today. You must be thirsty, Faye. I'll get you a cold drink before the concession closes."

"Thanks, Grandma." Faye had been about ready to share Robin's water bucket.

She was wrapping a shipping bandage around one of the pony's hind legs when a shadow fell over her. She glanced up. Catching a glimpse of a thin, pale face and silver-blonde hair, she hastily looked down again.

"Hi, Faye!" the girl said brightly. "Oh, Robin, you darling pony, that was absolutely fantastic."

"Hi, Nicole." Faye didn't bother trying to sound friendly. She clenched her teeth as Nicole stroked Robin's neck, murmuring softly to him. Smoothing the Velcro fastening closed, Faye shuffled to the pony's other hind leg and rolled a quilted cotton pad around it.

"Why don't you use shipping boots?" asked Nicole. "They're so much faster to put on."

"Because bandaging gives the legs more support and protection."

"Says who?"

"Lucy."

Nicole abruptly changed the subject. "You know, calling your grandmother by her first name is weird. I guess you think it sounds more professional, but it doesn't make any difference; everyone knows you're related."

Nicole was wrong but Faye didn't correct her. She wasn't about to explain that after the accident that killed her parents Faye had cried every time she'd said "Grandma," reminded of the mother she'd lost.

"Just call me Lucy," Lucy had said, gathering her close. She'd pulled Riley into the hug. "You both can, if it helps."

It had. A year or so later when they began saying "Grandma" again the Lucy stayed. It seemed right that someone who played so many roles in their lives should have more than one name.

Nicole's voice called her back to the present. "It's taking you forever to put on those bandages. You know, Andrew says shipping boots are just as good." Andrew Baumgartner was her very expensive and well-known riding coach.

Faye pretended to be too absorbed in winding the long stretch-cotton bandage over the quilt to listen. Nicole Walsh was an annoying know-it-all and it was pointless to even try to talk with her.

"Wow, were you ever lucky at that last jump," Nicole

went on, not realizing she was being ignored. "I thought you were going to eat that fence but Robin bailed you out. You are such a great pony, aren't you, Robin? You saved Faye's butt, didn't you?"

Faye had one quilt and one bandage left. Somehow she managed not to wrap them over Nicole's mouth. Instead, she crouched down beside Robin's off front leg. She hoped that by the time she was done, Lucy would be back with her drink so they could just load Robin and go home.

It would be early evening by the time they reached Armstrong and the farm. Kirsty and Riley would have the chores done so that all Faye would have to do would be to take care of Robin before falling into bed. She fastened the last bandage and stood up, exhausted after all the excitement of winning and very hungry, in spite of the heat. Maybe Lucy would stop at a fast-food restaurant on the trip home, just this once—

"Faye, did you hear what I said?" demanded Nicole. "We sold Silver Charms to California. That's why I didn't ride in the show."

"That's too bad, Nicole," Faye said. "He's a super pony. You'll miss him." She ran her hand down Robin's neck. He was already dry.

"Oh, Charms was too small for me. Anyway, we got a really good price for him so Dad can offer you more money for Robin."

Faye stiffened. "I keep telling you: he's not for sale!"

"You don't know how much money Dad's offering

Lucy for him. He won't even tell me. He says it's a small fortune and Lucy'd be crazy to turn it down."

"Then she's crazy, because she won't sell him to you!"

"Don't be so sure, Faye March," Nicole said, sticking out her pointed chin. "My dad says everything has a price."

Faye stared in horror at Nicole's smug face. Lucy had promised over and over that she'd never sell Robin and she'd always stuck to her word. But a small fortune…

Just last night Faye had come into the house after bathing Robin for the show and found Lucy hunched at the kitchen table glaring at a small mountain of envelopes with long windows, rising like a volcano above the hills of newspapers and horse magazines. "Bills and more bills," Lucy muttered in disgust.

Riley followed Faye inside, wiping his greasy hands on a rag. "The truck's ready to go. Gotta do something about those old tires soon. There's not much tread left on them."

Lucy rubbed her wrinkled cheeks. "And where am I supposed to come up with money for *tires*?"

"Look, I get paid at the end of next week—," Riley began.

"No, Riley, that money's for your college education. We'll get by somehow." Lucy noticed Faye hovering behind Riley. "Don't worry, Faye, it'll all work out."

Faye believed her. Money was usually in short supply at Hillcroft Farm, but Lucy always managed to make ends meet.

Now Faye looked down her long March nose at Nicole, squashing the seed of doubt the other girl had managed to sow. "Lucy will never sell Robin, not for any price."

Nicole narrowed her eyes and crossed her arms, preparing to argue.

"Nicole! Come here, darling," called her mother.

Both girls turned in the direction of her voice. Mr. and Mrs. Walsh had Lucy sandwiched between them at the end of the shedrow. Nicole ran to join them, shooting a triumphant glance over her shoulder at Faye.

Lucy was nodding, trying to squeeze past the Walsh family. They moved with her in a herd. Faye's stomach lurched as she watched her grandmother's bobbing head. What was Lucy agreeing to?

"She promised," Faye muttered to herself. "Lucy always keeps her promises."

"You might not ever get another offer like this again," Ken Walsh was saying loudly.

"Our little girl would be so happy," added his wife, Irene.

"Oh, please, Mrs. March," chimed in Nicole, "please let me have him. I'd take really good care of him."

"You know what? Don't give me an answer right now," said Mr. Walsh. "Just think it over, okay?"

"Okay," agreed Lucy, and Faye's world slipped sideways on its axis.

2

Faye's breath was stuck high in her chest. Panting for air, she pressed her face against Robin's neck, eyes squeezed shut to stop the waves of dizziness. The gabble of the Walshes' voices drifted away.

A cool hand settled on the back of her neck. "Drink this," said Lucy. She twisted the cap off a cold bottle of water and pressed it into Faye's hand.

"I feel sick to my stomach," said Faye.

"Too much sun," said Lucy. "Here, take off that helmet and get some water into you." She lifted the black riding helmet off Faye's sweat-soaked curls.

Faye took a long swallow of water. The cold liquid soothed her churning stomach. She took another drink and held the plastic bottle to her forehead.

"Feel better now?" asked Lucy.

Faye nodded. The ground was steady beneath her feet again.

Lucy hobbled to the back of the trailer and unfastened the door. "Come on, let's load Robin and get home to the farm."

"I saw you talking to the Walshes," blurted Faye.

"Uh-huh," said Lucy mildly. "Come on now, untie your pony."

"But—"

"Later, Faye. Pay attention to your pony right now."

Swallowing her impatience, Faye tugged at Robin's lead rope so the quick-release knot let go. The pony lifted his legs high in the shipping bandages as she led him to the back of the trailer. Robin reached out with his front legs and bowed down in a long stretch. He stood up with a full body shake, his heavy mane flying, and bunted Faye's arm with his nose.

"Okay, he's ready now."

She slipped the shank over his neck and positioned his head so he was facing directly into the trailer. Robin stepped up inside and rustled at the hay piled in the manger. Lucy snapped the trailer tie to his halter while Faye fastened the half door shut. She reached over and patted her pony's rump. "You're a good boy, Robbie. The best pony in the whole world."

Robin stamped a hoof, eager to get on the road to home.

Beside them, a huge diesel engine roared to life. A line of elegant hunters, turned out in matching stable sheets and shipping boots, paraded from the stables and loaded aboard a long, white gooseneck trailer.

"That's an aluminum trailer," said Lucy. "Weighs hardly anything on its own."

"That's what we need," said Faye. "Then our truck wouldn't have such a heavy load to pull." She reached into the truck box and scooped up her trophy.

Lucy snorted. "Girl, a trailer like that costs a fortune. If we could afford to buy an aluminum trailer we'd be able to buy a new truck as well."

They climbed into their battered old red pickup and quickly rolled down the windows to let out the heat. Lucy went through the long process of coaxing the tired old engine into starting. Faye settled the trophy in her lap and unbuttoned the collar of her riding shirt again. She caught sight of herself in the truck's side mirror. For once, her hair looked decent, the bushy curls tamed by her helmet and drying sweat. The image of Nicole Walsh's silvery straight locks came to mind. Faye scowled at her own red-haired reflection.

Lucy let the engine grumble for a minute or two. She tugged off her canvas hat and leaned back in her seat, groaning softly.

"Are your hips hurting again?" asked Faye.

Her grandmother nodded. "Always do after I've been standing all day."

"You should sit down more. That's why I packed that folding chair."

"I know. I forget to." Lucy lifted her sandy red hair with her fingers to cool her scalp. "Whew, it's hot in here."

Faye had to know. "You were talking to Nicole Walsh's parents."

"Uh-huh." Lucy wiggled the gearshift until it consented to shift into reverse.

Why was Lucy dragging this out? "And?"

"And they made another offer for Robin. A lot of money."

"What did you tell them?"

"What do you think? Faye, I wouldn't sell Robin without your say-so. Nicole Walsh will just have to find another pony."

Relieved, Faye sank back in her seat so Lucy could see in both mirrors to back out the truck and trailer. She should have known not to worry, but Nicole had gotten her spooked.

"You know, we just won a big class and a nice chunk of prize money. We should celebrate. How about if we grab some burgers from Arnold's on our way home?" asked Lucy.

"Can we get pizza?"

Lucy shook her head. "Takes too long. I don't want Robin standing in the trailer in this heat."

The money situation wasn't as bad as she'd feared, Faye realized, if they could still afford takeout burgers. As the pickup eased slowly backwards she watched the Walsh family slide into a shiny gold car nearby. Nicole held a cell phone to her ear.

"If we had a cell phone we could phone ahead for pizza," she said. It was going to take over an hour to get to Armstrong and her belly was rumbling.

Lucy snorted and straightened the steering wheel. The Walshes cut in front of them.

"And I could tell Riley about winning the junior championship."

"You can tell him when we get home."

"He'll probably be asleep, just like he was last night. Why is he sleeping so much?"

"Because he's tired out from working on the farm and putting in all those shifts at Arnold's."

"Lucy, if Riley's got a scholarship for university, why does he have to work at Arnold's so much?"

"He's got to have money for food and a roof over his head. That scholarship pays for his tuition and books and that's all."

"Good thing I'm going to be a professional rider," said Faye. "I won't have to bother with all that expensive college stuff. Right, Grandma?"

"Hmmm."

They were at the back of a long line of cars and trailers leaving the showgrounds. As they inched along, Faye watched Nicole stretch out on the back seat of her fancy car, chatting on the phone while she twisted a lock of silvery hair in her fingers. As far as Faye knew, Nicole had never mucked a stall or cleaned a saddle in her life. Grooms brushed and tacked her ponies for her and legged her up into the saddle.

"She probably doesn't even know how to put together a bridle," Faye grumbled.

"What's that?" asked Lucy, leaning forward to check for oncoming traffic. She slowly pulled out onto the road behind the Walsh car. Behind them a car honked. "Hold your horses, buddy, it takes us a while to get going." She shifted up a gear, carefully easing out the clutch so Robin wouldn't be jerked off balance back in the horse trailer.

Faye didn't repeat herself. She cracked open her window to create a breeze and slouched down in the seat. Closing her eyes, she replayed her jumping rounds inside her head. She dozed off, Robin's trophy cradled in her arms, as the old pickup and trailer crawled through the heavy weekend traffic out of the suburbs and onto the highway.

Lucy woke her as they pulled into Armstrong and turned onto the street leading to Arnold's Best Burgers.

"I'll go inside and get our food," Faye offered.

"No need for that. We'll go through the drive-through."

"But..."

It was too late. Lucy guided the truck and trailer into the narrow lane leading to the drive-through window. She shouted their order into the intercom and rolled ahead. Faye shrank down in her seat.

At the window, the server leaned out, studying the length of the truck and horse trailer. "Ma'am, are you sure you're going to be able to get through?"

Lucy handed the boy the money. "Of course I can! I've done it before."

The server shook his head and pulled back inside. Henry Arnold appeared in the window. "Lucy, what are you doing?"

"Getting supper, Henry, what do you think?"

"I thought we agreed you wouldn't take that truck and trailer through the drive-through, not after what happened last time."

"Henry, quit making such a fuss over a little dent or two in your building. My goodness, you're lucky I'm not holding you responsible for scratching up the paint on my trailer."

"Lucy, please…"

"Can't go back now, Henry. Got a lineup behind me. Don't worry; I'll take it slow. You should be thinking about widening this drive-through lane, like I told you." Lucy took the bag of burgers from the server and settled it on the seat. "See you, Henry. You take it easy, now."

Faye held her breath as the truck eased forward. Lucy shot her a quick glance.

"Now, don't let that Henry Arnold make you uptight, Faye. That man loves to worry about nothing; always did, even as a boy."

"He might be right this time." Faye peered over the dash of the pickup. The curve of asphalt between the cement-brick building and the black wrought iron railing wasn't very wide. "It doesn't look like we're going to fit."

"Of course we are!"

Faye saw people watching through the plate glass windows of the restaurant as Lucy manoeuvred the truck and trailer very slowly around the building. A man stood up, waving and pointing at the left wheel well of the horse trailer.

"Take it easy, fella, I've got at least an inch," muttered Lucy.

"An inch between the trailer and restaurant? That's all?" Faye squeezed her eyes shut and braced for the impact.

"You can open your eyes, Faye; we're all clear." Lucy chuckled at Faye's sigh of relief. "Told you I'd get us through."

She had. Faye looked out her window. The restaurant was indeed behind them. The old truck rolled through the parking lot and out the exit onto the street.

"Good driving, Grandma."

"Uh-huh. Slow and steady, that's the best way to handle things when you're in a tight spot, Faye. Don't get in a rush."

"Sure," said Faye through a mouthful of burger. "This tastes so good. Want one?"

"I'll wait till we're home." Lucy geared down for a stop sign. Robin stamped his hoof in the trailer behind. "Someone knows we're nearly there."

"He sure is smart. Probably one of the smartest ponies you've ever known, huh?"

"Probably," Lucy agreed, grinning.

They drove through the golden evening light along quiet, tree-lined streets. Faye waved to all the people Lucy knew so her grandmother could keep both hands on the steering wheel.

"There's Lydia Popowich—I don't know who she's with. Look how green her lawn is; she's got to be watering outside the sprinkling restrictions. Oh, it's Ethel Cairns and her grandkids. Make sure she sees you or her

23

nose will be out of joint. And here's Sam Desroches. On my side, Faye, that skinny fellow with all those fluffy little dogs. At least I'm assuming they're dogs; could be oversized hamsters except a man wouldn't be walking a bunch of hamsters, now, would he?"

"I don't think so," said Faye, "but you never know."

"That's right, Faye. When it comes to people you just never know."

As they left town, the yards became bigger and stretched out into fields. The road rose up, levelled off and climbed again. Lucy shifted down, the pickup's motor rumbling as it hauled the trailer up the grade.

Faye sat up in her seat, eager to reach the farm and show her older brother the trophy.

The hill steepened. The truck chugged slowly up it.

Lucy went down another gear. She let out the clutch. The truck surged forward with a roar. Leaning out her window, Faye waved to the Schmidt kids as they pushed their bicycles along the side of the road.

The truck slowed. Faye pulled back inside the cab. "Why are you stopping?"

"I'm not. Come on, old truck, don't quit on us now." Lucy shifted down again and pumped the gas pedal. The pickup was barely moving. She steered onto the shoulder of the road.

There was a loud thump from under the hood. The motor died. Lucy stomped on the brake.

"What's wrong?" asked Faye.

Lucy jammed the gearshift into first and yanked out

the parking brake, muttering under her breath. Faye caught a word she wasn't allowed to use, not even when she was dumped on her backside by a greenbroke three-year-old. Her grandmother puffed out her cheeks in a long sigh. "Looks like the truck's broke down."

"Oh no! So what do we do?"

"Guess we unload your pony and walk home. Good thing it's not much farther." Lucy opened her door and dug out her purse from behind the seat.

Faye slid out holding onto the trophy and the bag of burgers and slammed the door behind her. "What about the truck and trailer?"

"We'll have to leave it here. Hopefully, your brother can do some tinkering and get it going."

"Oh, Riley'll fix it, like he always does," said Faye. "He's a mechanical genius: you said so yourself."

"This breakdown might be beyond the skills of a nineteen-year-old," Lucy said grimly. She unfastened the trailer door.

Robin backed carefully out of the trailer onto the roadside. He looked about, no doubt wondering why they weren't at the farm, then dove at a clump of leafy green alfalfa. Faye let him rip off a mouthful before tugging him away.

"Let's ride home, Lucy." She slung the lead rope over Robin's neck, knotted it under his halter and led him alongside the wheel well of the trailer. "Come on, we can double. It's too far to walk." Faye slipped onto Robin's broad back.

Lucy passed her the burgers, trophy and purse. Stiffly, she hauled herself onto the wheel well and slung her leg over the pony's back, settling in behind Faye. She wrapped her arms around Faye's waist. "Sorry, Robin, packing the two of us home is a lot to ask of you."

"He doesn't mind," said Faye, "do you, Robin?"

Robin tossed his head, eager to get home. He marched up the hill, his pace slower than usual under the double load.

"I'll get off and walk if he starts to get tired," said Faye. "Oh, Lucy, isn't he incredible?"

"He sure is. A pony in a thousand."

"A million! At least."

"Let's just say he's a very special pony. He's going to be a hard act to follow when you outgrow him."

"What do you mean?" Faye tried to twist around to see her grandmother's face and hit her head on Lucy's chin. "I'm going to keep Robin forever. You said he was mine.".

"Sit still before we both fall off. Of course Robin's yours. I'm just saying you might want to start thinking about the next step."

"What next step?"

"Well, you're ready to start jumping higher fences."

"I know! I keep asking you to put them up."

"Faye, I'm not sure Robin has much more jump in him."

"Sure he does! Robin can jump anything."

For a moment, Faye thought about telling Lucy her

secret dream: riding Robin on the Olympic team and winning the gold medal. After all, a few other ponies had made it to the Olympics—Stroller, for example, although he'd been a few inches taller than Robin.

Before she could say anything else, Lucy spoke again. "Besides, you're growing, Faye. You must have noticed. Time'll come when Robin's going to be too small for you."

Her words felt like a bucket of cold water poured down the back of Faye's neck. Abruptly, she was aware that she could touch Robin's curved ears with her hands and that her heels dangled well below the curve of his belly.

"...move onto one of the bigger ponies," Lucy was saying.

I'll shorten my stirrups and go on a diet, Faye decided. *I will* not *grow too tall*. She vowed not to eat another Arnold's burger when they got home, no matter how hungry she was.

Unguided, Robin cut across the pavement onto the gravel road leading to the farm. He pricked his ears and broke into a rolling jog.

Faye felt a yank on her waist as her grandmother slid to one side. "Steady now," puffed Lucy, hoisting herself back into place. "Slow him down."

Faye leaned against the rope. "I'm trying." Robin shook his head against the pressure of the halter on his nose. "I should've put on his bridle. Hang on!"

The bay pony scooted into the farm's driveway, shaded by massive cedar trees. His hoofbeats echoed on the packed dirt. On either side, more ponies charged through the trees, running alongside the driveway behind rail fences, their long, thick manes rising and falling like the wings of birds. They whinnied shrill greetings. Robin called back, his tail flagging high.

The trees gave way as the driveway levelled off. Robin pranced into a wide area bordered by a huge red barn and a riding ring. Up at the old blue farmhouse the screen door slammed twice.

"Kirsty!" Faye said, recognizing the brown-haired girl running across the shaggy lawn after Riley. A yapping brown and white terrier bounded in front. Faye dropped the rope onto the pony's neck and held the trophy high. "We won the championship!"

"Faye!" Lucy reached around her and grabbed the rope. "Whoa, pony."

Robin sidled to a halt. Riley hurried over and wrapped his arm around Lucy's waist. "Hang on to me, Grandma. I'll help you off."

Lucy's knees buckled as she touched the ground. "Boy, it's been a lot of years since I've ridden bareback. Okay, okay, Stubby, it's good to see you, too." The terrier leaped into her arms, wriggling joyously.

Faye passed the trophy, the purse and the burgers to Kirsty and slid down.

"Wow, it's heavy." Kirsty stared at the gold figure of a jumping horse and rider atop a polished wood base. She read the words inscribed on the plaque. "Junior Jumper Champion. Who are all these names?"

"They're the past winners. Lucy'll get Robin's name engraved on one of the empty plaques."

"And yours, too."

"Riley, look at Robin's trophy," Faye urged.

Her brother flipped his dark red hair out of his eyes and peered over Kirsty's shoulder at the trophy. "Very nice." He smothered a yawn with his hand.

"*Nice*? Robin wins the Junior Jumper Championship and that's all you can say?"

"Faye, I'm proud for you and your pony but there's something that's kind of bothering me. Where's the truck and trailer?"

"Oh, the truck broke down. And we were nearly home, too."

"Broke down?" Riley turned to Lucy. "What happened?"

"It began to lose power coming up that last hill. I pulled over onto the shoulder of the road and there was a loud clunk. Then the motor died."

"It was a really loud clunk," added Faye.

Riley groaned, pressing his palm to his forehead.

"You will be able to fix it, won't you, Riley?" asked Faye anxiously. "We've got another show next weekend."

Riley dropped his hand and looked from Faye to Lucy. "I don't know. I'll have to have a look at it."

"Think it's something serious, do you, son?" asked Lucy.

"Uh-huh. This could be bad."

"My mom can give you a ride to the truck when she picks me up," suggested Kirsty.

"Thanks, but it's going to be dark soon. I'll wait until the morning," said Riley.

"But if you have a look at the truck right away maybe you'll find it's nothing serious and we won't be worried all night," said Faye.

Riley shook his head. "It's serious, all right, Faye. I don't have to look at it tonight to know that."

"But you'll have it running by next weekend, right?" persisted Faye.

Riley gave her a look. "Probably not. In fact, we'll be lucky if I can get it running at all—ever."

3

Faye heard a car rumble up the farm driveway as she was turning out Robin after an early ride. She slipped the pony's halter off his head and fed him a chunk of carrot. "That's got to be Kirsty," she told him. "Lucy's giving us an extra lesson together to make up for scratching from the horse show on the weekend because of the stupid truck. And I really wanted to go to that show! I know you would've won another championship. Anyway, I'm going to use Skylark in the lesson because it's going to be real simple stuff and you'd be bored."

Robin munched his carrot and listened politely.

"I wish Riley would hurry up and get that truck fixed," Faye sighed. The last time she'd asked him when the truck would be ready, Riley had thrown his wrench down and stomped away, leaving a shocked Faye blinking after him. That had been Friday, four days ago, and she'd hoped she could still get to the horse show. Since then, Lucy had forbidden her to say anything at all to her brother about the truck.

Robin bunted her hand. "Sorry, pony, that's all for now." Sighing, the bay pony sauntered away to join his pasture mates in the deep shade of the cedar trees. The sun burned deep blue highlights onto his russet coat. It was barely midmorning but already so hot that Faye's scalp prickled with sweat under the weight of her bushy hair.

Thank goodness Kirsty had finally arrived. They'd have their lesson together—sure to be a short one in this heat—and then maybe Kirsty's mom would drive them to the swimming pool in town. Faye slung the halter and shank over her shoulder and squirmed through the rail fence out of the pasture. Her boots thudded on the brick-hard ground as she sprinted along the footpath to the barn, the halter slapping against her ribs. The two brood-mares raised their heads from their grazing, their foals goose-stepping around them with bottlebrush tails held high. "Hey there, Blackbird, Grey Gull. Hi, kids!"

Blackbird's tiny filly whinnied and Faye laughed.

She broke through the grove of poplars behind the barn just as a sleek gold car rolled across the yard, a faint haze of dust pluming behind it.

Confused, Faye skidded to a halt by the tractor and swather as the gold car parked in the shadow of the old barn that rose like an ancient cathedral above all the other farm buildings. The elegant car certainly didn't belong to Kirsty's cash-strapped mother. Somehow, it looked familiar.

The driver cut the engine, and Faye heard a man's harsh voice through the open window. "This can't be the right place."

Mr. Walsh! Faye's heart sank in dismay. Through the windows of the car she spied two more heads—the rest of the Walsh family. What on earth were they doing here?

"It is," insisted Nicole, throwing open her door and scrambling out of the car. "I read the name on the sign. This is Hillcroft Farm."

Instinctively, Faye ducked behind the tractor. She peered around the rear wheel well.

Irene Walsh slid out of the front seat. She pressed a red-tipped finger to her chin and shook her head as she looked around at the tiny blue farmhouse huddled under an overgrown hedge of lilac bushes, the weathered rail fences and the huge barn with its arched roof stretching up into the sky. "My goodness, this place looks like something out of a low-budget western movie. That barn is so old it's probably a heritage building."

"The old lady must be short of money to let this farm get so rundown." Mr. Walsh got out. He crossed his arms, scowling. "How could she turn down my offer for the pony?"

"It wasn't enough. You've got to offer her more money, Daddy," said Nicole.

They were all out of the car now, wandering about the barnyard. Crouched behind the tractor, Faye realized she was trapped. If the Walshes decided to head up to the house she'd be discovered hunkered down among the weeds. How could she explain herself? Perhaps she could pretend to be suffering from a dizzy spell after running in the heat. She squeezed her eyes shut and willed the

Walsh family to get right back into their shiny car and leave.

"Oh, ick!" shrieked Mrs. Walsh.

"What is it?" demanded her husband.

"There's a pile of you-know-what! I nearly stepped in it with my new shoes."

Faye rolled her eyes. What was the big deal about getting a bit of pony manure on your shoes? It was just recycled grass, after all.

"Ken, let's go. No one's here," Mrs. Walsh said. "It's too hot to be outside."

"Mom!" protested Nicole.

"Sweetheart, we can phone Mrs. March. Come on, we'll go home and have a swim. We can stop for ice cream, if you want."

"I don't want ice cream, I want—look, someone's coming." Nicole pointed toward the farmhouse, then ducked into the barn.

The screen door at the farmhouse slammed. Stubby hurtled across the unmown lawn, yapping ferociously. Faye looked over her shoulder.

Lucy came down the veranda steps. She frowned at Faye, no doubt wondering why her granddaughter was crouched down beside the tractor while visitors milled about.

Faye seized a nearby thistle. She yelped as the prickles pierced her bare hands.

"What in heaven's name are you doing?" asked Lucy.

"Pulling thistles before they go to bloom."

"Faye, where's your sense? Use gloves or, better yet, a hoe. Now, who's here?"

"Where?" asked Faye, straightening. She pretended to notice the Walsh family for the first time. "Oh, we've got visitors."

Lucy shot her a sharp look before continuing on. "Irene! Ken! Good to see you. What brings you folks to this part of the world?"

"We apologize for just dropping in on you like this," said Mrs. Walsh, "but we were in the area and Nicole insisted on coming by to check on Robin. We heard you had to scratch from the show last weekend and she's been fretting about him."

"He's not in here," Nicole said, coming out of the barn with Stubby at her heels. "Oh, Mrs. March. How's Robin? He's not hurt, is he?"

The pounding of her own blood filled Faye's ears like a drumbeat. She couldn't believe the nerve of these Walshes, acting as if they had some kind of claim on her pony. Hands on her hips, Faye waited for Lucy to put Nicole in her place.

To her surprise, Lucy smiled kindly. "The pony's fine, Nicole. Our truck broke down so we had no way of hauling him to the show."

"Oh, that's good," sighed Nicole. "I mean, about Robin, not your truck."

"So what does the mechanic say about the truck?" asked Mr. Walsh.

"Well, looks like it needs a new motor."

Ken Walsh sucked in his breath between his teeth. "That'll be an expensive repair. You know, Lucy, once a vehicle starts breaking down you might as well get rid of it and get a new one. That's my advice."

Lucy smiled thinly. "Probably good advice, Ken, but a new truck isn't in our budget."

"I hope you've got a good mechanic."

"I sure do. My grandson, Riley."

The Walshes arched their eyebrows at each other.

Faye tapped her grandmother's arm. "How long will it take for Riley to put a new motor in the truck?"

Lucy shrugged. "I don't know. First he has to locate a motor. He's phoning auto wreckers right now."

"But what will we use for a truck?"

"Faye, we'll talk about this later. Right now, we've got company. Would you like to come inside for a cold drink?"

"Oh, I wonder..." Nicole hesitated, twisting a strand of pale hair around her finger.

"Go on," said Lucy.

"Could I see Robin? I'd really love to have a quick visit with him."

"Of course you can. Faye will take you to his pasture."

"Huh? But what about my lesson with Kirsty?" asked Faye.

"There's plenty of time. Besides, Kirsty isn't even here yet."

"She will be, any minute now, and I've got to catch Skylark."

"It won't take much time to take Nicole to Robin's field. You can bring Skylark back with you."

"I can find him myself," said Nicole, "if it's too much trouble for Faye to show me."

"I'll take you," said Faye grudgingly. She stomped back up the path, Nicole running after her.

"Is something wrong, Faye?" Nicole panted when she'd caught up.

Faye didn't answer. Stubby shot past, yipping at a figure pushing a bike up the driveway.

"Faye, wait up," called Kirsty. She dropped the bike beside the road and ran to catch up with them. "Sorry I'm late. My mom was late this morning so she couldn't drive me." She scraped her brown hair off her sweaty forehead. "Wow, it's roasting." She looked at Faye, waiting for her to introduce Nicole.

"Better hurry up and get Lancelot ready," said Faye.

"Okay, but..." Kirsty tipped her head at Nicole.

Faye sighed. "Kirsty, this is Nicole Walsh."

"Hi, Nicole!" Kirsty grinned at her. She'd been to only a few horse shows as Faye's groom and obviously didn't remember who Nicole Walsh was, even though Faye had complained about her many times. "Are you here to buy a pony?"

"Sure, if Faye'll sell Robin!" Nicole giggled, pretending she was kidding. "I tried out a couple of ponies this morning but they just weren't what I want."

It dawned on Faye that Nicole was dressed to ride in breeches, paddock boots and a pale blue polo shirt.

"That'll never happen," laughed Kirsty, believing Nicole was joking. "Faye will never part with Robin."

A sly smile spread over Nicole's thin face. "We'll see."

Faye clenched her jaw.

"Well, I've got to get my pony ready for our lesson," said Kirsty. "Nice to meet you, Nicole." She jogged to the barn.

Faye and Nicole walked in silence the rest of the way to the pasture. Robin was resting in the shade of the trees with his buddies. "There he is," said Faye.

"Can't we go in? I want to pet him."

"I'm in a hurry. I've got a pony to tack up." Skylark was grazing on the other side of the field.

"That's okay. You catch your pony. I'll see Robin by myself." Nicole slipped through the rail fence.

Faye ducked through after her.

"Oh, are you coming with me?" asked Nicole, weaving around the clumps of droppings dotting the sunburned grass. "You really don't have to."

"Oh, yes, I do," muttered Faye.

"I don't understand why you don't keep Robin in a stall."

"Because he likes to be out with his friends," said Faye.

"But what if he gets kicked and injured?"

"It hasn't happened so far and we've been turning him out all his life."

Nicole sniffed. "If he were *my* pony I wouldn't take such chances with him. Hello, Robin, you sweet boy.

Oh, yes, I'm glad to see you, too."

To Faye's dismay, Robin nickered at the sound of Nicole's voice. He nuzzled at the other girl's hands. Nicole fished a sugar cube out of the pocket of her breeches and gave it to him without asking Faye's permission.

Cupboard love, Faye thought sourly. Robin was only interested in Nicole for the treats she brought him.

Nicole wrapped her slender arms around the pony's russet neck and hugged him tightly. "I miss you, too." She let go and stepped back. "You're so beautiful. But look, your lovely hair is getting bleached by the sun."

Faye moved in front of Nicole. She scratched Robin between the jowls, his favourite spot. The pony closed his eyes in bliss.

"You know, Faye, you're not being fair to Robin," said Nicole.

"What?"

"He's such a talented pony. He deserves to compete at the big shows—Thunderbird in Langley, Spruce Meadows in Calgary, the Royal Winter Fair in Toronto. You can't afford to take him to those shows, can you?"

Faye didn't say anything. They both knew the answer.

"You're being selfish, do you know that, Faye?"

Faye glared at Nicole with her perfect straight, pale blonde hair, silver-grey eyes and name brand riding clothes. Nicole had everything...except Robin, and she wasn't getting him.

Nicole ignored Faye's sour look. "We'd give him the

best care," she went on. "The very best money can buy. Can you do that for him?"

"Robin's happy here. With me."

The pony tossed his head, annoyed at being crowded by another pony.

"It's time to leave him alone," said Faye firmly. "He wants to rest."

She moved off a few steps and waited for Nicole. She was prepared to drag the other girl away if she had to.

She didn't. Nicole kissed Robin's muzzle and cooed her goodbyes. She picked her way across the pasture, exclaiming over the weeds and parched grass and rails chewed toothpick-thin by pony teeth until Faye wanted to turn around and kick her in the shin with her boot.

Faye knew a lot of things needed fixing around the farm, but there just hadn't been time—or money—this summer. Lucy had been trailering her and Robin and a couple of the sale ponies to shows, and Riley was working full-time flipping burgers at Arnold's for the summer. It was hard just to get the everyday farm chores done, even with Kirsty's help.

"I thought you had to catch a pony," said Nicole when they were nearly at the barn.

"Skylark! I forgot him!"

"My goodness, Faye, you need to get organized."

"I am! I just have a lot of things to do."

She left Nicole shaking her head and hurried back to the pasture. Skylark was still on the farthest side of the pasture. Faye trudged across the width of the field, the dry grass crunching beneath her boots. The silver-grey pony lifted his head and watched as she approached.

"Don't even think of running away," Faye told him. Skylark could sometimes be hard to catch.

Skylark strolled off, his long white tail swishing over his flanks. "Whoa," called Faye. She slapped the pockets of her jeans, searching for a tidbit to entice him to stand still until she got the halter over his head. All she found was a shrivelled piece of carrot.

She held out her hand palm up, offering the piece of carrot. "Skylark, please stop!"

Abruptly, Skylark swung around, his tiny ears snapping forward. He sighed as Faye slid the lead rope around his neck and gave him the dried-out carrot.

"Good boy," Faye said, sliding the halter on him. "I'll get you a better treat, I promise. Come on, let's go." She chirped and tugged on the rope.

Skylark followed her to the gate, dragging his toes. Faye clucked, trying to get him to move faster. She wanted to get back to Lucy and the Walshes quickly. Nicole was up to something; Faye could feel it in her bones.

"Hurry up, Skylark," Faye urged. The pony flicked his tail and ambled along beside her down the path. As they came out of the poplars, everyone turned towards them.

"Well, here he is," said Lucy. "Good-looking pony, wouldn't you say, Ken?"

"They all look the same to me," said Mr. Walsh. "All I know is one end bites and the other end kicks." He chuckled at his own humour.

"That's Robin's brother?" said Nicole as Faye led Sky-lark to the barn. "He's not even the same colour."

"His half-brother. They have the same dam," explained Lucy. "Faye, stand him up for us, please."

Suddenly, Faye caught on. Lucy was trying to get the Walshes interested in buying Skylark. She posed the pony, clicking her fingers in the air to get his attention. Skylark arched his neck and pricked his ears forward.

"Oh, he looks beautiful," said Kirsty, coming out of the barn.

"He sure does," Faye agreed. Okay, you had to look past the grass belly and wind-tangled mane and tail, but what horse person wouldn't be thrilled with his sturdy body and clean legs? She glanced over her shoulder at Nicole, trying to read her expression.

Nicole let out a long breath. A sigh of admiration?

"Well, what do you think, honey?" asked Mrs. Walsh.

Nicole shook her head sadly. "I'm sorry, Mrs. March, but he's just not Robin."

"Try him out, Nicole," said Faye. "He's really nice to ride. Just like Robin."

"I'll get his saddle and bridle," offered Kirsty.

"Go ahead and ride the pony, sweetie," said Ken Walsh.

"But he's not what I'm looking for."

"Come on, Nicole, you've got to ride at least one of these ponies."

"No, Daddy, I don't want to!" Nicole swung on her heel and stomped over to the car.

Mr. Walsh rubbed his chin. "Lucy, can we talk?" He walked over with Mrs. Walsh into the shade of the poplars. After a moment, Lucy followed.

"These people are weird," hissed Kirsty. "What do you suppose they want to talk to Lucy about?"

"They're probably trying to buy Robin," Faye replied glumly. She led Skylark into the barn.

"What?" Kirsty snorted. "Well, that'll never happen." She slipped into Lancelot's stall.

"You don't understand. The Walshes are *rich*." Faye put Skylark in the stall beside Lancelot and lifted down a plastic caddy of brushes.

"Yeah, so what? It'd take more than money to get Lucy to break her word to you. You told me that she promised you a long time ago that Robin would always be yours."

Faye picked up a rubber curry. "It's just that the Walshes won't give up, no matter how many times Lucy says no. Nicole acts as if Robin's already hers."

"Well, he's not. Faye, you've got to stop worrying so much. Get rid of that negative attitude."

"You know, you're right. Lucy'll never sell Robin, no matter how bad things get around here."

Kirsty's face appeared in front of Skylark's stall. "What do you mean? What's wrong?"

"Riley can't fix the truck. It needs a new motor and Mr. Walsh said it would be expensive."

"So what does Mr. Walsh know about fixing trucks? He was probably trying to scare Lucy so she'd get worried about money and sell Robin."

Faye stared at her friend. "He doesn't know my grandma very well, then, does he? *Nothing* scares Lucy March."

Outside the barn, car doors slammed and an engine started. Kirsty darted to the barn door and peeked out. "They've gone! Yeah! Oops, here comes Lucy."

"Aren't you two ready yet?" Lucy called from the doorway.

"Just about," called Faye, hurrying into the tack room with Kirsty. "We'll be right there!"

Kirsty was right, Faye realized as she packed her saddle and bridle to Skylark's stall. She was getting upset over nothing. She had to learn to ignore Nicole and her troublemaking. When Faye rode Skylark behind Kirsty and Lancelot into the ring a short while later, she decided she wouldn't ask Lucy a single question about her talk with the Walshes.

Lucy leaned against the white board fence with Stubby at her feet in a shadowed corner of the ring, studying the girls as they walked and trotted their ponies in circles and serpentines. "Faye, your shoulders are slumped—*again*. Sit up, girl! Kirsty, step deeper in your heels to keep your lower legs from swinging. That's it, you've got the idea. Keep working."

Stubby yipped softly as Riley slouched over to the fence. Shaking his dark red hair over his forehead, he handed Lucy a scrap of paper. Lucy scowled and pinched the bridge of her long nose.

Faye trotted Skylark up to them. "Did you find a motor, Riley? Are you going to have the truck fixed by next weekend?"

Riley widened his eyes. "Are you kidding?"

"Then when will you—"

"Not right now, Faye," said Lucy sharply. "Go work on leg yields. Make sure you have him moving off that right leg."

"But—"

"Faye, please!" pleaded Lucy.

Faye blinked at her, astonished. Lucy never begged. She turned Skylark and walked off, glancing back over her shoulder. Riley paced back and forth in front of Lucy, waving his hands about.

Something was going on, but what? Faye had to know. She circled Skylark to pass close to them, hoping to overhear their conversation, but as she drew near, Lucy pressed her finger to her lips to shush Riley.

Faye heard nothing but Skylark's hooves thudding on the packed sand as she rode by them. Then, a few strides past, she could make out the hum of their voices again.

In spite of her new resolution, worry buzzed at Faye like a persistent mosquito, waiting for just the right moment to bite. She changed direction, trotting Skylark towards her grandmother and brother from the other side. This time they didn't notice her.

"...got to do something!" Riley was saying urgently.

Lucy's head was down, resting in the crutch of her hand. The thump of the grey pony's footfalls muffled her unusually soft reply.

"…just don't know anymore," Faye thought she heard her grandmother say. Abruptly, she swung Skylark around to face them. "What's going on?"

Riley's eyes slid to Lucy. The old woman lifted her head, sandy eyebrows arched. "Have you got that right leg yield sorted out?"

"Yes, but—"

"Show me. On the three-quarter line."

"I want to know—"

"Come on now, Faye. Concentrate on your riding."

They're not being fair! Faye fumed as she trotted Skylark along the short side of the ring, preparing to turn between the middle and the outside fence. *They treat me like a little kid.*

She pressed her right leg firmly on the pony's girth, asking him to move sideways. Skylark resisted, tensing his sides and tossing his head, so she nudged him with her heel. With a sigh, he gave in to the pressure of her leg and stepped with his right hoof under his body, carrying them over to the outside rail on a diagonal line. Engrossed in her thoughts, she didn't notice Kirsty cantering Lancelot up beside her until they nearly collided. She pulled Skylark away just in time.

"Sorry, Faye," said Kirsty, breaking to a trot.

Faye shook her head. "It was my fault. I should have been looking for you."

"Faye, pay attention!" yelled Lucy. "Get your head out of the clouds and concentrate on your job. Honestly, I don't know where your mind is at these days."

Faye let Skylark shuffle to a halt. Kirsty pulled up beside them. Lucy looked up at the two shocked faces staring at her and closed her hooded lids over her eyes. "I'm sorry. I shouldn't have shouted at you."

"That's okay," muttered Faye.

"My mom gets cranky in the heat, too," said Kirsty helpfully.

Lucy smiled thinly. "Yes, it is very hot. Let's call it quits for today before somebody ends up with heatstroke. You girls can put the ponies away." With Riley at her side, she made her way to the house.

Faye and Kirsty sat side by side on their ponies, watching Lucy and Riley leave.

"What's going on?" asked Kirsty.

Faye shrugged and shook her head.

"Well, it's sure got Riley upset. And Lucy...I've never seen her look so worried. You'd better find out what's up, Faye."

"But you told me I was worrying about nothing!"

"I was wrong." Kirsty kicked her feet free of the stirrups and swung down from Lancelot's back. "Something's happening, Faye, and it's not good. I can feel it in my stomach. It's the same feeling I had just before my parents told me they were getting divorced."

Faye stared at her in dismay. What else could possibly go wrong?

4

The telephone started ringing as Faye tugged on her socks. By the third ring she realized no one was answering and rushed out of her room and down the stairs. Halfway down, she heard the answering machine come on.

"Should have let the machine get it in the first place," she grumbled, trudging back upstairs. It was nearly eight-thirty and she still had to comb her hair—always a time-consuming task. Where were Lucy and Riley and why hadn't they woken her up?

The answering machine message ended and a man's voice came on. "Lucy? It's Reg calling back. Look, I'm sorry but things are tight around here, too. I can't take you up on your offer of that good mare. Best of luck. Hope things get better soon."

Halfway up the staircase, Faye paused, confused. What mare? They had only geldings for sale, unless you counted the yearling and weanling fillies. That had to be it. This Reg didn't know a young female horse was called a filly until she reached five years.

The phone rang again. With a groan, Faye leaped down the stairs two at a time and snatched it up. "Hillcroft

Farm, Faye speaking."

"Oh, hi, is Lucy March there?" asked a woman.

"No, she's not. Can I take a message?"

"Hmm, sure. Can you tell her Nancy Davidson phoned back and we've already found a pony for our son."

"Sure, Mrs. Davidson, I'll let her know." Faye hung up and pulled out the dry-erase pen from the jar beside the phone. The cap was missing. She tried a few practice strokes but the dried-out pen would make only faint smeary marks on the whiteboard.

Stubby began to yelp outside, the monotonous barking he made when a stranger or other undesirable person (the same thing in his suspicious doggy mind) came close to the house. Lucy shushed him sternly.

Faye dropped the useless pen back in the jar and went out onto the veranda. Lucy stood at the end of the lawn with a man carrying a briefcase. He wore light tan chinos with a well-pressed crease down the middle, gleaming brown loafers and a dark green polo shirt with words embroidered in gold thread on the pocket.

"Lucy! Got a message for you."

Lucy waved her hand to show she'd heard. She turned back to the man with the briefcase. "I haven't quite made up my mind, Mr. Dunstan."

"Herb, please. I understand completely. It's a big decision, especially when you've lived here so long. I just thought I'd come by after your call yesterday and introduce myself, go over some numbers, maybe help you clarify your thoughts."

"Appreciate that, Herb."

"Okay, then. You take some time, have a good think about things and I'll call you in a few days."

Herb Dunstan shook Lucy's hand and eased himself into a dark green SUV with gold lettering on the sides. As the big vehicle turned around, Faye made out the words: *Valley Wide Real Estate.*

Lucy pulled herself up the veranda stairs and settled into a bent willow chair. She eyed a tub of pink petunias drooping in the corner. "Look at that. Just a day without water and those flowers are wilting. Boy, do we need rain."

"Who was that man? Why was he here?" demanded Faye.

"First, what message do you have for me?"

"A Nancy Davidson said to tell you she's found a pony for her son."

"Figures." Lucy shook her head.

"Now will you tell me why that man was here?"

Riley came around the lilac hedge packing a hammer and a plastic jug full of nails. "Got those rails back up, Lucy, but the yearlings have just about chewed right through them. We're going to have to get some new rails pretty soon. Hey, fuzzy. What happened to your hair?" He tugged her curls.

Faye swatted his hand away. "Nothing! I just haven't brushed it yet. Riley, a real estate man was just here."

"Oh?" His face went blank. He set down the nail jug and boosted himself onto the railing.

Faye narrowed her eyes at him. "You knew about this. Why didn't you say anything?"

Riley plucked at a hole in his jeans. "Lucy, you've got to tell her."

"Tell me what?" Faye spun around to face her grandmother. "Lucy, what's going on? Tell me. Please!"

"Okay, calm down. Faye, nothing's for certain yet. I want you to keep that in mind."

"What do you mean?"

"I'm thinking about selling the farm."

Faye blinked at Lucy, stunned. Had she heard her grandmother right? Her ears were filled with a strange buzzing that seemed to be vibrating from inside her head. Something was wrong with her hearing. Lucy couldn't possibly have said that.

But even as she stared into her grandmother's dull green eyes, she knew that she had.

Faye shook her head. "You can't do that. This is our *home*."

Lucy said nothing. She looked over at the old barn rising above the rest of the farm buildings, its arched roof reaching to the sky. Inside the house the mantel clock chimed the hour. The metal roof pinged overhead as the sun crawled across it, and a foal whinnied.

"Grandma! Listen to me—you can't sell our farm. Riley, tell her!"

"Faye, we don't have a choice," her brother told her.

"What do you mean?"

"We're in trouble. Big trouble. We have a lot of bills

and no money to pay them. We have to do something."

"But…how can we have no money? Are we poor?" She thought of the fridge full of food, the hayloft stuffed with bales. She recalled the horse shows she'd competed in all spring and summer before the truck had broken down. Entry fees were expensive; she'd heard Lucy complain every time she wrote a cheque to pay for them. How could they have gone to so many competitions if there wasn't any money?

"No, Faye, we're not poor, not exactly," Lucy said finally, "but we're in a really bad situation. We need to buy hay and put a new roof on the barn and now we have to fix the truck."

"What about a loan from the bank?"

"Got one earlier this spring. We're having trouble meeting the payments. Girl, we just don't have any money coming in."

"But why didn't you tell me?"

"Didn't want to worry you. I never thought it'd get this tight."

"There must be something we can do! Maybe sell one of the ponies?"

Lucy snorted. "I've been on the phone for two days calling everyone I know. Can't get any interest. Oh, maybe next month or in the fall, but it'll be too late then. We need money *now*."

"How could you have let things get so bad?"

Lucy bowed her head, covering her eyes with one hand.

"Back off, Faye," growled Riley. "Grandma's done her best to keep the farm going."

"What do you care, Riley? You're always complaining how much work the farm is. I bet you're happy we're losing it."

"You're a spoiled brat, Faye March, do you know that? Lucy works day and night to keep this farm going so you can play around with ponies."

"Kids, please don't fight," said Lucy weakly.

Faye couldn't ignore Riley's last remark. "I do not play with ponies! I work *hard* at riding because I'm going to be the best."

"Enough of this Olympic rider crap! You're not a little kid anymore. It's time for you to grow up and quit being so selfish."

"Selfish? I'm not selfish!" shrieked Faye.

"You sure are. Lucy's prepared to give up everything important to her just so she won't have to break her promise. The farm and all the ponies. Even Blackbird."

Faye shook her head. "No, Grandma wouldn't sell Blackbird. Would you, Lucy? You raised her, you won all those ribbons on her and she's given you all those good foals. You wouldn't get rid of her."

"And what would she do with a broodmare in town?" said Riley before Lucy could speak. "Because that's where we'll have to live after the farm is sold."

"Riley, that's enough." Lucy sat up in her chair, her shoulders square.

"She should know, Lucy."

"Grandma, is he right? Are we going to move into town?" Faye stared at her grandmother in dismay.

"It won't be so bad. We'll board Robin out, maybe someplace with an indoor arena so you can ride inside all winter."

"I don't care about an indoor arena. I don't want to leave the farm. I love it here."

"I don't want to leave either, Faye, but I don't know what else to do." Lucy's eyes were suddenly very bright.

"Well, I do," muttered Riley, "but you won't listen to reason."

Lucy held up a hand. "No, Riley. Don't say it."

"But it would save everything!" Riley swung his legs over the railing, jumped onto the lawn and stalked off.

"What's he talking about?" asked Faye. "How can we save the farm?"

Lucy shook her head. "We're not going to do it."

"Why not? Grandma, we've got to try!"

"Faye, no!"

"I don't understand. What's wrong with Riley's idea?"

"I made you a promise. I won't break my word." Lucy caught her hand and held it tight, her bony fingers binding Faye's tightly.

"What do you mean...oh, no." Faye swayed as understanding dawned. Lucy's grip held steady. "He wants me to sell Robin to Nicole!"

A hard squeeze of the knobby fingers. "Now don't you fret. We'll find some other way. Come into the house. I need more coffee. Have you had breakfast yet?"

"I'm not hungry." Faye pulled her hand free. "Is he right?"

Lucy pushed herself to her feet. "Is who right?"

"Grandma, you know what I'm talking about. Is Riley right? Would it be enough money to save the farm?"

"Child, don't you worry about it. Everything's going to be okay. There'll be changes, but we'll get through them."

"Would it be enough money?" Faye persisted. "Tell me. I need to know."

"Yes. Selling Robin would give us enough money to pay off our debts and have some left over. But don't worry; I'm not going to sell him behind your back. He's your pony, Faye."

Faye felt herself petrifying, starting with her heart. She turned around on heavy feet.

"Where are you going? Faye, are you all right?"

She paused at the bottom of the veranda stairs. "I'm... fine, Lucy." She said the words because she wanted her grandmother to leave her be. The truth was she really didn't feel anything at all. What could you expect from a stone heart?

"Faye, come back here and get your shoes on."

Her stockinged feet slapped along the familiar path to Robin's pasture. Blackbird whickered as she passed by the mares' field, her filly's whinny a shrill echo half a beat later. The sounds bounced off Faye's stony armour.

She slipped through the pasture fence. Robin lifted his head as she stumbled over the damp grass toward him. She leaned on his sturdy shoulder, pressed her face into his mane. Robin laid his head over her shoulder in a pony hug. She waited to feel the comfort that her pony's solid presence always brought.

It didn't come. Her heart remained a heavy weight inside her chest. The other ponies crowded around, tiny muzzles bunting at her pockets, fluted nostrils puffing gusts of warm air on her neck. Robin flattened his ears and they scattered away. Tail swishing, he meandered up to the fence, rolling one eye in her direction. Faye climbed the fence and slid onto his back. The slightest squeeze of her calves and the pony trotted across the field. The other ponies followed, their hooves drumming on the sun-baked earth. Robin sprang into canter. Faye bent forward, twisting her hands in his mane, urging him to a gallop. His breath came in sharp grunts, his hind legs grabbing at the ground to propel his body through the air. Then they were at top speed, wind-tears blurring Faye's eyes, the landscape flying past in a long smear of colour. Her brain took a nanosecond to register tall, dark shapes as they burst into the woods, tree branches smacking her face as Robin dodged between them. She crouched lower, melding herself to the pony's body.

The pasture fence materialized in the leafy shadows. Robin checked his stride, his ears swivelling back for directions. And because she could feel nothing, not even fear, Faye tapped her heels against his sides and urged him on. He hopped forward, gauging the height and breadth of the obstacle in his path. His head and neck reared up in front of Faye. She dug her fingers deeper into his mane. The pony's hocks kicked out behind him, flinging her onto his neck. She glimpsed the top rail of the fence beneath them, so close she could make out the pattern of the bark. Robin dropped down, his front legs stretching out to find solid ground.

She was sliding down his neck, the curved ears coming closer. She braced against her hands and tried to push herself back. Her left hip shifted, slipping onto the pony's shoulder, pulling the rest of her body over the side.

Robin veered to the left and pitched his rider into the centre of his back.

"Thank you," Faye whispered, the wind shredding her words. Was that a warm flicker of affection she felt or just the body heat from her galloping pony?

They charged on into the mountains.

It was early afternoon when Kirsty found them. She rode Lancelot into the clearing and slid from his back. "Faye? Oh, thank goodness you're all right."

Or was she? Robin hovered over his partner, curled in a ball on the rocky ledge at the edge of the clearing. He tipped an ear in Kirsty's direction but didn't stir, his chin resting protectively on Faye's shoulder.

Kirsty tied Lancelot to a sturdy tree with the rope attached to the halter he wore under his bridle. If Lucy and Faye hadn't taught her to keep the halter on for trail rides, she would have tied him by the bridle reins, which could easily break. She'd learned so much from them over the past months; there was still so much more she wanted to know.

Faye didn't move as Kirsty hurried over the sparse grass to her. She knelt down, trying to see her face through a curtain of tangled curls. Faye's eyes remained shut, even when Kirsty said her name.

"Are you hurt? Tell me where. Please, Faye, say something!"

The curls quivered. "I'm not hurt."

The slab of rock was hard against Kirsty's knees. She shifted to a more comfortable position. They'd come to this place before on their rides and once for an early morning picnic. The March family had stopped here many times, had even carved their initials in the rocks.

"Lucy and Riley are worried crazy about you," she said. "They've been looking everywhere."

No response. Kirsty noticed Faye's feet were in stockings but no boots. How many times had her friend warned her about the crushing force of a pony hoof on bare toes?

"Faye? Riley told me about the farm." Kirsty swallowed, a lump in her throat blocking the words she wanted to say. "I'm so sorry," she managed to croak.

The tangled head lifted. "It's going to be okay," rasped Faye, her voice muffled.

Kirsty looked away. Her eyes stung with tears. Faye was plainly sick with grief about losing the farm yet she was offering Kirsty reassurance. "Oh, Faye, I wish there was something I could do to help!"

"There's nothing, Kirsty. It's all up to me."

"What do you mean?"

Faye didn't answer. She pushed herself into a sitting position, wrapping her arms around her knees. Robin leaned his forehead against hers. A single tear dribbled down her cheek and plopped on the rock slab.

Kirsty could feel her own tears starting to fall. She tried to squeeze them back in, wanting to be brave and supportive for her friend, not a blubbering mess. She felt Faye's hand rubbing her arm, offering comfort, and collapsed in a storm of weeping.

"Please, Kirsty, don't cry. It's going to be okay."

"Why do you keep saying that?" Kirsty sobbed. "It's going to be terrible! You're going to move, the ponies are all being sold and I don't know where I'll keep Lancelot. I know, I'm the most selfish person in the world worrying about myself and my pony at a time like this."

"No, you're not. You're the best friend in the world."

"You're my best friend, too, besides Lancelot. Oh, Faye, I don't want anything to change!"

Faye's hand gave a quick squeeze and fell away. Kirsty's tears passed. She wiped her face dry with the back of her hand. Robin had moved away to graze the ragged grass and Faye was looking out over the valley below. Kirsty followed her gaze.

Below them the mountain fell away in a cascade of rocks. Kirsty knew if you shimmied to the very edge of the rock face and leaned over, peering through the trees, you could make out the arched silver roof of the old barn at Hillcroft Farm. Copying Faye, she hugged her arms around her legs and propped her chin on her knees. A soft breeze buffeted her face. A crow flapped past, swivelling a dark eye in their direction.

"I can't bear to lose all this," she whispered.

"We aren't going to," replied Faye.

"Oh, Faye, you've got to get real. There's no money."

"There will be. Soon. Lots of money."

"What are you talking about?" Kirsty studied her friend with concern. Faye was behaving very oddly, her voice flat and dull. Had she been hit in the head with a branch or even fallen? "Are you going to win the lottery or something?"

Faye frowned and shook her head. "Don't be silly." She paused, taking a deep breath. "I'm going to sell Robin."

"What? Are you nuts?"

"It's the only way."

"But...you can't."

"I can. Or Lucy can, if I tell her to. Kirsty, I've made up my mind. It's the only way to save the farm—our home—and I have to do it." Faye's shoulders trembled.

"Oh, Faye, are you sure?"

"No, but what else can I do?"

"To Nicole Walsh?"

Faye twisted her lips in a bitter smile. "Who else?"

"This is terrible! I just can't believe it's happening."

"Look, Kirsty, this is really hard. I don't want to talk about it anymore. Please." She got to her feet and went to

Robin, guiding him by the mane to a fallen log. "We'd better go back now."

Kirsty scrambled up and untied Lancelot. Slipping her foot into the stirrup, she bounced up into his saddle. "Something will happen, Faye, it just has to. Wait a few more days. Lucy will find the money somehow. She won't let you sell Robin; I know she won't. Please, don't just give up."

Astride Robin, Faye smoothed his black mane. "I'm not giving up, Kirsty. I'm growing up."

And before Kirsty could say anything more, she set her pony on the trail home.

5

They came for Robin the very next day.

"So soon?" Faye said when Lucy told her the Walshes would be at the farm first thing in the morning. She'd expected to have a few days with Robin to say goodbye.

Lucy wrapped her arm around Faye's shoulders and squeezed. "Nicole wants to get him right away."

"And Nicole always gets what she wants," said Faye bitterly.

Lucy rubbed Faye's shoulder. "I know this is tough for you…"

She jerked away. "I don't want to talk about it."

Faye spent the night in a sleeping bag in Robin's stall. She'd been awake for hours, combing Robin's mane and tail and polishing his coat to a russet sheen, by the time Kirsty arrived.

"I'll do the chores," Kirsty said, peering into Robin's stall. "You stay right here."

"Thanks," mumbled Faye, grateful for every second she had with her pony.

She stepped up onto an overturned bucket and slid

onto Robin's back. He shifted nervously, sensing her agitation and distress. Faye pushed those feelings away and focused on how solid and warm her pony felt beneath her. She flopped down onto his neck and let her arms dangle along his shoulders. Comfort wrapped around her like a quilt on a cold night. Robin sighed and cocked a hip, dozing off in the front corner of his stall.

Outside, an engine rumbled up the driveway to the farm. Faye covered her ears. The sound grew louder. Ponies whinnied and Stubby yapped.

"Wow," said Kirsty from the open doorway of the barn.

Faye sat up. She nudged Robin up to the stall door. Craning her neck she could see a narrow sliver of the world outside the barn. A huge, indigo blue dually truck towed a long, white horse trailer into the yard. Nicole burst out of the back seat of the truck, without waiting for the rig to come to a full stop, a package tucked under her arm.

"Where is he?" she demanded. "I want to put these shipping boots on him to protect his legs."

"You should try him out first." It was Lucy's voice. "You've never ridden him."

"I'll ride him when I get him home. I already know he's exactly what I want."

"I really think Nicole should ride Robin before you buy him. Just to be sure," said Lucy. She had to be talking to Mr. and Mrs. Walsh, Faye realized.

"Oh, she's sure, all right," said Ken Walsh. "Nicole's

made up her mind that this is the pony for her."

"We're on a tight schedule today, Lucy," said Irene Walsh, glancing at her slender gold watch. "Nicole has a piano lesson at eleven."

"All right then, we'd better pay you for this pony," said Ken Walsh. He pulled a cheque out of his pocket and passed it to Lucy.

"So where is Robin? Where's my new pony?" Nicole bounced on the balls of her feet. "I'm so excited he's finally mine."

Robin whinnied inside his stall.

"That's him, isn't it?" Nicole rushed into the barn, pushing past Kirsty. She unlatched the stall door and flung her arms around Robin's neck, dropping the package to the floor. "Oh, you darling." She looked up at Faye. "Would you please get off my pony?"

Faye slid to the ground.

"Look, Robin, I've bought you new shipping boots to protect your legs in the trailer." Nicole ripped open the package and began fastening the tall, canvas-covered boots around the pony's legs.

Faye drooped against the stall wall, watching Nicole in horrified fascination.

"Are you okay?" whispered Kirsty anxiously.

Faye shrugged. She didn't seem to feel much of anything.

"There, Robin, you're all set." Nicole straightened, her face glowing pink. She turned to the other girls. "Doesn't he look good in navy blue?"

Already Robin looked unfamiliar in the knee-high shipping boots. He bunted Faye gently with his tiny muzzle. She scratched under his jaw and he pressed his head against her.

"Please don't let him do that," said Nicole. "Andrew says it's bad manners for a pony to rub his head against a person."

"He's not rubbing his head," said Faye. "He wants to be scratched—"

"I said: don't let him do that."

Faye stepped back.

"Thank you," said Nicole primly. "Now I need his halter."

"Here it is." Kirsty reached outside the stall for Robin's halter and shank.

"Oh, you can keep that old thing. Daddy bought me a brand new leather halter for Robin. I'll get it."

In a daze, Faye watched Nicole buckle a stiff leather halter with a gold name plaque on Robin's head. She took a firm grip on the matching leather shank and brought him out of the stall.

The pony turned his head as he left Faye, his nostrils fluttering. She reached out and her fingers brushed over his velvet flanks.

"Robin, quit that," said Nicole with a snap of the shank.

Faye's teeth chattered. She clamped her jaw tightly.

Outside Riley showed Mr. Walsh how to open the back doors of the horse trailer.

"Just picked it up yesterday," Ken Walsh said. "Nothing but the best for my little girl's pony."

"We're ready, Daddy," called Nicole. "Blue looks good on him, doesn't it, Mom?"

Irene Walsh nodded. "Very nice, dear."

"I'm going to get him a blue sheet. You'll like that, won't you, Robin?"

Faye knew Robin hated wearing blankets of any kind. Somehow he always managed to slip out of them, even when all the buckles and snaps were done up securely.

Nicole walked the pony up to the trailer. Robin paused, stretching out his neck and snorting softly at the strange interior.

"Come on, boy, it's okay." Nicole tugged on the shank.

Don't go! Please, Robin, don't go! Faye's heart gave a huge thump, kick-starting her nervous system. Her limbs trembled as panic flooded through her. This couldn't really be happening. Robin couldn't be leaving. "Lucy," she quavered.

Her grandmother's strong fingers grasped her shoulders. "Steady, Faye. He's going to a good home."

Faye's hope for rescue dissolved like sugar in water. She felt a stabbing in her chest as her heart shattered. Deep inside, she'd always believed Lucy would never let Robin leave, that at the very last minute her grandmother would realize that selling him was completely wrong and stop the sale in its tracks.

It wasn't going to happen. Robin stepped up into the

trailer, his hooves clopping on the thick rubber-matted floor. He waited patiently while partitions and doors were fastened. Faye willed him to kick up a fuss, lash out with his sharp hooves and strong teeth and behave so badly the Walshes would demand their money back then and there.

Lucy released Faye to shake Ken Walsh's hand. "Thank you so much," he boomed. "You've made my daughter a very happy girl."

They climbed back into the truck. Doors slammed and the engine started. The Walsh family waved merrily from behind tinted windows. The truck and trailer slowly moved forward.

The world tilted. Riley grabbed Faye's arms. "Hey, are you okay?"

Faye bobbed her head, her mouth open wide as she forced air into her lungs. Her eyes were fixed on the horse trailer vanishing into the trees lining the driveway. Tearing free of Riley's grasp, she dashed into the barn and scrambled up the ladder into the hayloft. On her hands and knees she crawled over the stacked hay bales to reach the opening in the arched ribs of the roof. She leaned out, clutching the frame, to catch one last glimpse of the trailer hauling Robin away from her.

She could see nothing but trees.

Heedless of splinters, she let her hands slide down the wood frame. She slumped onto a bale.

"Faye?" Kirsty knelt beside her. Her hazel eyes were shiny with tears. She squeezed Faye's hand.

Kirsty's voice came from far away. The strange, in-a-dream feeling had settled over Faye again, blocking the pain the way the snowmobile suit she wore in winter to do chores kept out the cold. Insulated by its fuzzy fog she sat with Kirsty for a long time.

The rattle of the old metal wheelbarrow being pushed along the alley below roused her. She staggered to her feet.

"Where are you going?" asked Kirsty as Faye picked her way back over the hay bales.

"There's work to do," she said hollowly.

"Oh, Faye, you don't have to. Lucy and I will take care of the chores."

Faye shook her head and climbed down the ladder.

"Where do you want this?" Riley stood in the entrance to Robin's stall, holding an empty water bucket.

"Just stick it in the feed room." Lucy spoke from inside the stall. "I'll scrub it out later."

Riley turned and saw Faye. He reached out an arm. "Hey, how're you doing?" Faye twisted out of his hug and went inside the stall. She took the fork from Lucy.

"Faye, I can do this," said her grandmother.

"Look, why don't you take off for the day with Kirsty?" suggested Riley. "I bet Mrs. Hagen'll give you a ride into town. You could go swimming at the pool, have ice cream."

Faye shook her head. "I want to do this. Please. Leave me alone."

They left. Faye slumped against the wall. A single tear

trickled down her cheek and dripped on her boot. Faye stared at the bright blob of moisture, waiting for other tears to fall. Her eyes burned but no more tears fell.

She pulled herself upright with the fork. Stabbing the fork into the shavings, Faye cleaned her pony's stall for the last time.

6

"Faye?"

"Hmm?" She hadn't noticed Lucy come into the tack room.

"I said: are you up to riding in the Valleyview show this Saturday?"

Faye rubbed glycerine soap into the leather cavesson dangling on the metal bridle hook that hung from the ceiling. She shrugged. "I guess so."

Lucy's brow creased. "You don't have to, you know. It's just a schooling show and it's only been two weeks…"

Since Robin left, Faye finished for her silently. Two weeks or two years: Faye knew that time was never going to make a difference. She would always feel a sharp stab of pain at the loss of her partner.

"Well?" Lucy prompted.

Faye realized she'd drifted off again. "I'll ride." She rinsed the tack sponge in a bucket of water and wrung it out thoroughly.

Lucy stood up a riding boot that had fallen over. She lingered for a few moments, watching her granddaughter's hands deftly slip the cavesson onto the headstall of the bridle and fasten the buckles. "Well, all right, then. We'll go."

Saturday morning, at a time when most people were still stretching in bed, Faye stood outside the jumper ring at Valleyview Stables and tried to memorize her course. Luckily, it was the same course for both ponies she was riding—Skylark and Sparrow. The problem was she couldn't seem to make it stick in her brain, even after walking it twice with Lucy.

"Let's go through it one more time," said Lucy. She stood in front of the course diagram tacked to a large piece of plywood nailed to a post.

Faye turned to study the brightly painted jumps arranged around the smoothly harrowed sand. "White brush box heading towards the in-gate. Left turn to the blue and white vertical and the grey wall and then…" She chewed her lip, trying to remember.

"Right turn to the red planks," Lucy reminded her.

"Oh, yes, the red planks." Faye recited the remainder of the jump course.

"You got it. Now, where are you in the order of go?" Lucy scanned a list of numbers penned on a large whiteboard by the in-gate. "Fifth in. That'll give you a chance to watch some other riders go around the course." She checked her watch. "Time to get Skylark warmed up. Remember it's his first show. He may need extra work to settle him down."

"I know, I know." Why was Lucy fussing so much? Usually it was Faye who was wound up at a horse show.

Kirsty had groomed and tacked the silver-grey pony. She held his reins as he dozed, slack-hipped, beside the horse trailer.

"I walked him around for a bit," said Kirsty, passing the reins to Faye, "but he kept falling asleep."

"He may come alive yet, when he gets in the warm-up ring with all the other ponies," Lucy warned.

Faye pulled down her stirrups and swung aboard. Skylark ambled over to the warm-up ring, gazing with mild interest at the strange horses and riders milling about. The activity seemed to give him enough energy to keep his eyes open. Obediently, he walked, trotted and cantered when asked and plunked over a few low jumps. Faye suspected his placid approach to life was rooted in a lazy disposition. Acting up would simply take more energy than Skylark was willing to put out.

Robin had been a handful to ride at Skylark's age, she remembered; she'd had to pay attention every second she was on his back. More than once she'd been caught off guard and found herself sitting on the ground after he'd bucked or spun around, startled by an open umbrella or a flapping plastic bag. Channelled into jumper training, those same lightning-quick reflexes had made him a champion, clocking jump-off round times seconds faster than his competitors'.

Skylark was a pleasant pony to ride but Faye was certain he would never make a top competitor. He was just too laid-back.

"Number thirty-nine!" the whipper-in called from the

jumper ring. "You're on deck."

"Faye!" Kirsty's voice pulled her out of her reverie. "It's your turn."

A palomino had jigged out of the ring by the time Skylark and Faye reached the gate.

"Go right in," said the whipper-in.

Faye glanced over at her grandmother for last-minute instructions.

"Good luck," said Lucy.

Skylark shuffled into the ring. He raised his head and slowed, gawking at the unfamiliar jumps.

"Come on, Skylark, they're just the same as the jumps at home," Faye told him.

The judge blew the whistle to begin their round. Faye kicked Skylark into a canter and steered him at the white brush box.

The grey pony slowed, leery of the solid white obstacle he was headed for. Faye drummed her heels against his sides, wishing desperately for her crop. Why had she forgotten it? Skylark inched towards the jump, folded his legs tight to his chest and crept over it in slow motion.

He landed and broke to a walk, throwing Faye up onto his neck. She pushed herself up and dug her heels in. Skylark veered towards the in-gate. Faye pulled him away.

Slowly, they rolled over the sand. Faye recognized many of the people lined up on the rail watching. Lucy's scowling face leaped out at her. "Pay attention!" she hissed.

Faye jerked her mind back to the job at hand. There was only one direction to go. She turned Skylark left and the blue vertical lay right in their path. She glanced down at the number two at the foot of the right standard just to be sure.

Skylark eased over the low jump and trundled along to the wall, painted to resemble grey stones. Impressed, he bounced up and cleared the wall by a couple of inches.

They cantered on towards the end of the ring. Skylark's ears flicked back, waiting to be told which way to go. Faye tightened her right rein, twisting her head to look over her shoulder to find the track to her next jump. She couldn't spot it. Oh no, she was going the wrong way. She swung the pony left. Where was the next jump?

Right there, just a few strides out of the corner. Skylark cantered to the green and white oxer and bounded over it.

Dimly, Faye was aware of a whistle squealing. Skylark was nicely lined up for the green coop. He was rolling along well, keeping up a good pace and looking for his next fence.

They jumped the coop and cantered on.

The people outside the ring waved their arms. The whistle blew again. Faye pulled Skylark up.

"You're off course!" bellowed the judge.

"Huh?" Faye looked back at the maze of colourful jumps, bewildered. She hadn't gone off course for years, not since she was six years old.

"Clear the ring, please. Next rider!"

Sick at heart, Faye guided Skylark out the gate. Where had she gone wrong?

She ran through the course again. Brush box, blue vertical, wall…red planks! She'd turned the wrong way after the wall.

Dazed, she slid off Skylark's back. She stroked the silver-grey neck. "Sorry, boy." Even though he'd gone at a snail's pace he'd jumped clean and honestly and she'd let him down.

Lucy approached. Faye braced herself for the scolding she was about to get.

"I'm sorry, I don't know why—"

"Oh well, that was too bad," said Lucy mildly, patting Skylark. "He was jumping good."

"Don't be upset, Faye," said Kirsty, taking the pony by the reins. "It could have happened to anyone."

"But I never go off course."

"Well, it's not the end of the world, is it?"

Faye opened her mouth to protest and shut it. Kirsty was right; going off course wasn't the end of the world. *That* had already happened.

"You might as well take the pony back to the trailer," said Lucy. "You've got a long wait until his next class."

Faye followed Kirsty and Skylark back to the trailer, where Sparrow waited. Skylark held his head high as he walked alongside Kirsty, an extra spring in his step. He was right to be proud of himself, Faye thought, patting the solid neck. *He* hadn't screwed up. She sighed and tried to muster some enthusiasm for riding flighty

Sparrow next.

Skylark stopped abruptly and whinnied. Somewhere in the trailer parking area, a shrill whinny answered.

"Whoa! Walk, will you?" A girl in a black helmet sawed on the reins of a plunging bay pony as he shot out from between two trailers. They vanished into the crowd.

Faye's heart lurched. She stood on tiptoe, trying to see over the horses and riders passing in front of her.

"What is it, Faye? What do you see?" asked Kirsty. The crowd parted and she gasped. "That's Robin! Oh no, what's wrong with him?"

Robin's neck was bowed, his mouth gaping to escape the heavy pressure of the bit in his mouth. His tiny ears lay flat against his head and his heavy black tail whipped back and forth as he hopped sideways along the rough track of the parking area.

"Andrew!" wailed Nicole from Robin's back. "Do something!"

A wiry man appeared and seized the pony's reins. Nicole slumped in the saddle. The man patted the fidgety pony's neck and led him towards the warm-up ring. Faye and Kirsty followed after them. Once they were in the ring Andrew Baumgartner released Robin.

"Okay, trot him around to settle him down," he told Nicole. "Loosen the reins and let him move out."

Nicole's face was paper white under the black brim of her helmet. Her silver eyes fixed straight ahead, she slid an inch of rein through her gloved fingers. Robin broke into a jerky, high-headed trot. Nicole squealed and snapped back the reins, yanking the bit in Robin's tender mouth. He threw his head in the air to escape the pain and slid to an abrupt halt.

Faye clapped her hand to her mouth as if she'd just been hit in the gums with a metal bar.

"Don't jerk on his mouth!" Andrew roared.

Nicole burst into tears. "He won't do anything right! I can't get him to behave."

"Oh, honey, are you all right?" Mrs. Walsh picked her way through the sand in her high-heeled sandals, her summer dress fluttering.

"Andrew, just what is going on here?" demanded Ken Walsh, striding over to the trainer.

Faye squeezed into an opening on the rail.

"...bad case of nerves," she heard Andrew say.

"Nerves?" shouted Mr. Walsh. "Why is she nervous? It's only a little backyard show. On that pony she can beat these kids with her eyes shut!"

A bitter taste filled Faye's mouth at the sight of Robin. His bright russet coat was dulled with sweat. His tail swished over his flanks. He stomped a front hoof and Nicole squawked with alarm. She kicked her boots out of her stirrups and jumped down.

"Andrew, I want you to warm him up for me."

"Nicole, you can do it," said the trainer.

"No, I can't," she pouted. "He just won't do anything for me!"

"You both have to get used to each other. Come on,

get back on."

"Andrew, I think it would be a good idea if you rode the pony," said Irene Walsh. "Just to settle him down."

Faye gazed at Robin's vacant saddle with longing. She ducked under the rail and stood beside him. In her dark riding jacket with her red hair stuffed out of sight under her helmet, no one recognized her.

Except Robin. The tiny ears snapped forward. He nickered softly.

"Hey, ponyboy," murmured Faye.

Robin tugged at the reins, struggling to touch Faye. "Come on, stand still," protested Nicole. She looked over at Faye and her silver eyes grew round.

"Nicole's going to have to learn to handle the pony sooner or later," said Andrew.

"Andrew's right," said Nicole sharply, her gaze fixed on Faye. "I'm the one who should be riding Robin."

"Oh, darling, are you sure?" said Mrs. Walsh.

"Quit nagging, Mom."

Andrew boosted her back into the saddle. Taking a deep breath, Nicole gathered up the reins, shortening them until Robin's head nearly touched his chest.

The pony's eyes were on Faye, imploring her to do something. "Don't hold the reins so tight," she whispered to Nicole. "He doesn't like it."

"Don't tell me how to ride *my* pony!" Nicole slammed her heels into Robin and he bounded away.

A hand tugged at Faye's arm. "Faye, talk to her!" said Kirsty. "Tell her not to be so rough with Robin."

"I tried! She won't listen."

"Oh, this is horrible."

Robin trotted frantically around the perimeter of the ring, his mouth gaping wide to escape the constant squeeze of the bit, while Nicole bounced up and down in the saddle. Faye shook her head, bewildered. She'd never seen Nicole ride like this before. What was wrong with her?

"Here comes Lucy!" cried Kirsty.

"Stop that! Stop right now, young lady!" Lucy shouted to Nicole, shaking her fist as she hiked across the warm-up ring. "Quit being so rough with that poor pony's mouth. How is he supposed to do anything with you hanging onto his reins like that?"

Nicole hauled Robin to a stop and gaped at Lucy. "You're not my coach!"

"Darn right I'm not. If a student of mine had such heavy hands—"

"You ripped us off, Lucy March!" shouted Mr. Walsh, stomping up. "This pony is a dud!"

Lucy went rigid. Sandy head raised high, she turned to face Ken Walsh. The activity in the warm-up ring slowed. Riders pulled up their mounts and coaches moved closer. Andrew Baumgartner jogged through the churned sand after his client, Irene Walsh mincing in his wake.

"Now, Ken, let's just take it easy," said Andrew.

"What's to take easy?" Ken Walsh roared. "I spent a small fortune on a pony my daughter can't even ride. The old woman cheated me!"

A hushed gasp ricocheted around the warm-up ring.

"*Mr.* Walsh! The pony you bought from me is a top-class jumper. Any of these people around us can tell you that, including your own trainer. Isn't that right, Andrew?"

"Well, uh, the pony has won a lot of ribbons in the jumper ring," said Andrew Baumgartner. He held up the palms of his hands. "But, hey, everyone can have a bad day, even an animal."

Ken Walsh rounded on him. "Baumgartner, you told me my girl would win everything on that pony. That's what I paid the big bucks for! What did I get? A crazy animal my daughter's scared to ride!"

"Robin is not crazy!" yelled Faye.

"Nicole, sweetie, please get down off that pony," pleaded Irene Walsh.

"No!" hissed Nicole, darting a look at Faye. "I'm going to ride."

"I want my money back," demanded Ken Walsh.

"Daddy, no," Nicole wailed.

Faye's heart leaped. Robin would be coming home. She was going to get her pony back.

"Now, Ken, calm down," said Andrew. "Maybe we need to rethink our game plan. You know, back off the competition aspect until Nicole's used to the pony."

"Daddy, don't you dare send my pony back!" shrieked Nicole. Robin trembled, pinning his tiny ears.

"Sweetheart, your father is worried about you," said her mother.

"You said I could have any pony I wanted," snuffled Nicole. "I want *this* pony. I want Robin!"

Raking his fingers through his hair, Ken Walsh paced down a small circle of sand. "All right, all right. You can keep the pony. But just for a few more weeks. If he doesn't shape up soon, he's gone." Grim-faced, he marched out of the ring.

Faye hurried to Lucy. "Grandma, what's going to happen? What does Mr. Walsh mean by *gone*?"

"I don't know," Lucy replied tersely. "Come on, it's time to saddle Sparrow. He's going to need lots of riding to settle down."

Faye trotted after her grandmother. "But about Robin—are you going to give them back their money? Is he going to come home?"

"Faye." Lucy shook her head. "You know most of that money has been spent on the new truck and paying the bills."

"But if Nicole can't ride Robin, what will happen to him?"

"Lucy! What was *that* all about?" Shrill voices demanded Lucy's attention, drowning out Faye's last question. She sighed as a small group of curious onlookers swarmed her grandmother.

She went to the horse trailer and slipped into the rear compartment where the ponies travelled. She sat by herself on an overturned bucket for a long time, trying in vain to think of a scheme to rescue Robin.

"There you are." Kirsty poked her head in the trailer.

"Are you okay?"

Faye shrugged. "How can I be? Robin saved Hillcroft Farm and now look how he's being treated. It's all my fault. I shouldn't have let Lucy sell him to Nicole."

"You did what you thought was the right thing."

"I was wrong."

Kirsty didn't say anything, but her eyes told Faye she agreed.

Faye got up. "We'd better get Sparrow saddled. He's going to need lots of riding to settle down."

Sparrow was wildly excited to be at his first horse show. He dashed around the warm-up ring, hurdling the low fences like a steeplechaser. Faye rode on automatic pilot, her attention diverted by Nicole's struggles with Robin.

She reined Sparrow to a walk and watched, dismayed, as Nicole grimly aimed the fussing bay pony at the practice jump. Robin heaved awkwardly over the obstacle, unable to stretch out his neck and head for balance because of Nicole's death grip on the reins. He landed and jerked his head to escape the jab of the bit against the bars of his mouth. Faye winced, feeling his pain.

Nicole shook her head in frustration.

"Release, Nicole!" shouted Andrew. "Release the reins over the jump! Okay, try again. This time hold onto the mane."

Nicole flushed pink. Holding a hank of mane over the jumps was a technique a beginner rider used to prevent hurting her pony's mouth with the bit until she learned to release the reins.

She slowed Robin, pretending to adjust her feet in the stirrups. Faye knew she was delaying another attempt at the practice fence. To her surprise, Nicole moved Robin up beside Sparrow. Faye looked away.

"Please help me. Faye, you've got to."

Something in the tone of her voice made Faye glance back. Nicole's face was as pale as candle wax. "I...I don't know what you mean," said Faye, bewildered. What could she do for Nicole that Andrew Baumgartner, with his years of experience and international reputation, could not?

"Yes you do! Give me the secret. Please, I need it," begged Nicole.

"What secret?"

"Oh, don't pretend you don't know what I'm talking about. The secret to getting Robin to jump!"

Faye stared at her. "There's no secret." Didn't Nicole realize it was her own riding that was causing the pony's jumping problems?

"Faye!" Kirsty beckoned from the gate "It's your turn. Come on!"

Nicole grabbed Faye's arm. "Please. Tell me!"

"But I don't have any secret to give you! I didn't do anything special; I just rode him, that's all."

Nicole dropped her hand, slumping in the saddle.

"Look, maybe if you loosened the reins—," Faye began.

"I can't! If I let go of the reins he'll run away."

"Hurry, Faye," Kirsty called.

"Nicole! I'm waiting," said Andrew. "Take the jump again."

Scowling at Faye, Nicole booted Robin into a canter, then sawed on the reins to slow him down.

"Faye! Get a move on! They're holding the gate for you," barked Lucy, appearing beside Kirsty. Faye hustled Sparrow over to them.

"Grandma, look what's happening with Robin."

Lucy dragged her hand over her face. "Faye, you've got to put Robin out of your mind. You're on Sparrow now. This is his first competition and he needs your full attention."

Aghast, Faye looked down at Lucy, hardly able to believe what she'd heard. How could her grandmother be so heartless? Faye couldn't just forget her partner when he was obviously miserable. Over her grandmother's shoulder, she saw Robin scurry past, his russet neck and shoulders slick with sweat, his heavy tail lashing like an angry cat's. Her heart ached for him.

"Faye, I know this is tough on you but you've got to focus. Either go into that ring and ride Sparrow with all your ability or put him away," Lucy said sternly.

Like a summer squall sweeping over the mountains, anger stormed through Faye. "This is all your fault! If you hadn't lost all our money Robin would still be mine. He saved the farm and look how he's being treated! And you won't do anything to help him."

She dug her heels into Sparrow and galloped away.

"Hey, slow down!" said the whipper-in as they barrelled up to the gate of the jumper ring. "Number forty? Go right in; we've been waiting for you."

Sparrow trotted two strides into the ring and stopped dead, goggling at the unfamiliar jumps, the people leaning on the fence, the plywood booth that housed the judge. Faye stiffened her jaw.

"Get up now," she said briskly. She squeezed her legs against his sides. Sparrow resisted, unsure about these strange surroundings. She clucked with her tongue and gave a sharp nudge with her heels. He shot forward, snorting, as Faye steered between the jumps, letting him have a good look before they began their round.

The whistle blew and Faye's world narrowed to the sand-covered ring cluttered with brightly coloured obstacles. As surely as if there'd been a line traced in the sand, she rode a straight path to the brush box. Sparrow hesitated and she reached back and tapped him with the whip. The youngster shifted gears and flew over the jump. Faye turned him to the second fence. They bounced over and rocketed up the line to the third, leaving out an entire stride. Faye rode by instinct, all of her senses and skill engaged in staying with the agile pony. The wind whistled in her ears as Sparrow bounded over the course in double time, clearing the jumps with feet to spare. After the final fence, Sparrow galloped a full circuit of the ring before Faye could persuade him to slow to a walk.

The crowd at ringside burst into applause. Sparrow arched his neck proudly and pranced from the ring. Faye patted him and murmured praise, her blood still pounding through her veins.

"That was amazing!" Kirsty ran up to them. "He went so fast. How did you stay on?"

Faye shrugged. "I just did."

Kirsty rolled her eyes. "You make it sound so easy."

"I can't explain it. I just do it, that's all."

A moment later, the clapping ceased as Robin shuffled in, ears flicking and nostrils flaring. Under her black helmet Nicole's face was ghostly pale. She licked her lips and slid her hands up the reins.

"Oh, don't do that," breathed Faye. "Looser, not tighter."

Robin shook his head against the unyielding hold on his head. Without waiting for the judge's whistle, Nicole slammed her heels into the pony. Robin leaped into canter. The judge hurriedly blew the whistle and Nicole turned to the first fence. Murmurs swelled from the onlookers as the pony charged at the low jump. Faye was dimly aware of heads turning in her direction, of Robin's name whispering through the crowd. Her eyes were fixed on the bay pony galloping over the sand. Nicole clung to his mane as he launched himself over the jump and rushed around the turn to the next.

Faye sank her teeth into her bottom lip. Robin was going much too fast, sand flying up from his hooves as he skittered around the corner. He bore down on the bit, trying to drag the reins free, then abruptly threw his head in the air, knocking Nicole squarely in the face.

Blood spurted from her nose. They crawled over the second fence and galloped on to the third.

Robin's stride stuttered. Barely a length from the jump he skidded to a stop. A soft gasp rose from the crowd.

Nicole swung Robin away from the jump. She swiped at her nose, smearing blood across her upper lip. She squared her shoulders and turned the pony at the fence again.

Robin planted his feet, ears pinned, and refused to move toward the jump. Nicole banged her heels against his ribs. The pony whirled around, bolting across the ring before she could pull him up. She turned him back. Tail lashing, Robin jogged sullenly forward, creeping to a halt five strides out from the jump.

The judge's whistle blew. Robin and Nicole were eliminated.

"He stopped," Faye whispered, stunned. In all their years together, Robin had never refused a jump.

"Mr. Walsh is going to be really mad now," said Kirsty.

Jerking the pony around, Nicole galloped from the ring. She barged through the gate, glaring fiercely at the protesting whipper-in.

Andrew Baumgartner and the Walshes surrounded Nicole and Robin outside the ring. Heads turned as they passed by en route to the Walshes' horse trailer. Faye stood up in her stirrups looking for Lucy and sighted her grandmother heading in the direction of Nicole's entourage. Finally, her grandmother was going to do something to save Robin.

A couple with a small girl stepped into Lucy's path. To Faye's dismay, her grandmother stopped to talk with them. She groaned as Lucy turned back, bringing the little family with her.

"Girls, this is Isabelle. She would like to try out Skylark."

Faye ground her teeth in frustration. Of all the times for pony buyers to come looking!

"He looks like such a gentle pony," said Isabelle's mother.

"He is that," agreed Lucy. "He'll make a super pony for a beginner."

"Oh, Isabelle's not a beginner," said the father. "She's had riding lessons for over three months now."

"Well, that's a good way to start. Come and meet Skylark." Lucy herded the family toward the horse trailer.

A diesel engine roared to life. A dark blue dually truck pulling a huge aluminum trailer pulled out of the parking area. The Walsh family was leaving, without taking the time to cool out Robin or put on his shipping boots.

"Number forty! Faye March!" The whipper-in ran up and handed her a ribbon. "Didn't you hear the results on the loudspeaker? You got fourth place!"

The little girl, Isabelle, gazed up at the yellow strip of fabric dangling from Faye's fingers. "You're so lucky," she said solemnly. "I wish I was you."

7

When they returned to the farm Riley was waiting for them, perched on the top rail of the corral and whistling in the midsummer dusk while Stubby rustled in the grass. He slid down off the fence and helped unload the ponies. Then he handed Lucy a scrap of paper. "She's phoned three times. Wants you to call her back right away. She said it's really important."

Lucy squinted in the dimming light at the paper. "Oh boy, now what?" Whistling to Stubby, she stumped over to the house.

"I wonder what all those phone calls are about," said Kirsty as she and Faye led Skylark and Sparrow across the barnyard.

"Probably more trouble," said Faye gloomily.

"Maybe Isabelle's parents have decided to buy Skylark."

"That would be good news." Faye swung open the gate into the ponies' field. Propping it against her hip, she unbuckled the chestnut pony's halter and slipped it off. Sparrow shook all over, his golden mane and tail flying, then gently snuffled her face. She rubbed the tiny white star on his forehead. "Yes, you were a very good boy. Now, go have a nice roll. You deserve it."

"And you were wonderful for Isabelle," Kirsty told Skylark. She let the grey loose and the two ponies sauntered away into the darkness. "Faye, I was wondering: if you sell Skylark will there be enough money to buy back Robin?"

That possibility hadn't even occurred to Faye. "Oh, I don't know! There could be. Kirsty, wouldn't that be fantastic?"

"Let's ask Lucy right away. Maybe all those phone calls were from the parents."

Faye was already running back along the path. Above the barn door the light illuminating the yard flicked on and there was Lucy looking about. She turned at the sound of pounding feet.

"There you are," she said to Faye. "I've got something to tell you."

Faye's battered hopes pulled themselves up again. "We've already figured it out," she said. "Skylark's sold so now Robin's coming home." She felt a surge of gratitude; dear, steadfast Skylark had ambled to the rescue just in time.

"I knew it would all work out," cried Kirsty.

Lucy squinted against the glare of the yard light. "Just what *are* you two talking about?"

"Isn't that what you're going to tell us? That Isabelle's parents are buying Skylark so now we've got the money to buy Robin back?" asked Faye. She glanced uneasily at Kirsty. "Weren't all those phone calls from Isabelle's parents?"

"No, Faye, they were not," said Lucy. She puffed out her cheeks in a long sigh. "I don't know how to say this so I'm going to come right out with it: Nicole Walsh is bringing Robin here—"

"She doesn't want him anymore? She's giving him back?"

"No, Faye! Nicole is coming with Robin."

"What?"

"She wants us to help her with him. She figures we know Robin better than anyone else, since we're the folks who raised and trained him, and we can work out what's gone wrong with him."

"But there's nothing wrong with Robin—you know that! It's Nicole!"

"Her father is running out of patience. If Robin doesn't perform better for Nicole soon, he'll be sold."

"Why are we helping Nicole, then? If they're going to give up on Robin can't we buy him back?"

"Faye, I tried, but Ken Walsh isn't going to let us have that pony back."

"Why not, if Nicole can't manage him?"

"I get it," said Kirsty. "If you got Robin back and were winning on him again it would make Nicole look bad."

"But…that shouldn't matter."

"It does to Mr. and Mrs. Walsh," said Lucy.

Faye was silent, confused by a belief that appearances were more important than ability or improving skills.

"How long will Nicole be here?" asked Kirsty.

"Just a week. Her parents are going away on a business trip. She was going to be alone at home except for the housekeeper." Lucy sighed heavily. "A week isn't going to be much time."

A week of Nicole Walsh sounded like forever to Faye.

Give me the secret, Faye! Nicole's plea echoed through Faye's brain. Was that why she was coming to Hillcroft Farm—to learn a secret that didn't exist?

"I know this is going to be tough on you," continued Lucy, "but remember: you wanted me to do something to help Robin. If we help Nicole we're making Robin's life easier. Okay?"

Faye shrugged.

"When's she coming?" asked Kirsty.

"Tomorrow morning. Bright and early, whatever that means to Ken Walsh."

8

Nicole stopped in her tracks in the middle of the yard. "We're going to sleep in a barn?"

Hunched under a mound of luggage, Riley bumped into her. "Hey, get going."

"But…a barn!" Nicole swung around to Lucy.

"That's where the kids always have sleepovers in summer," Lucy said firmly. She put her hands on Nicole's shoulders and spun her back. "In the hayloft."

"Oh my goodness, I don't know about this," murmured Irene Walsh. "Perhaps the spare bedroom?"

"We don't have one."

"And you wouldn't want to sleep in Faye's room," added Riley. "It's a health hazard." Smirking at his sister, he sidled around Nicole and shuffled to the barn.

"Should we trip him?" muttered Kirsty.

Faye shrugged and hoisted a duffle bag.

"You're right," said Kirsty, "then we'd have to carry all Nicole's stuff ourselves." She surveyed the pile of luggage in the back of the Walshes' truck. "Why *is* there so much? If I packed up my entire bedroom I couldn't fill all these bags."

Faye smiled dutifully. Kirsty was trying hard to relieve the tension.

Loaded with luggage, they waddled by Nicole and her mother like a pair of overburdened pack mules.

"You don't have to do this," Irene Walsh said to her daughter.

"I *want* to stay," Nicole insisted. "It'll be fun sleeping in a hayloft."

"You should be training with Andrew this week," grumbled Ken Walsh. He lowered his voice. "Now, if that pony gives you any trouble at all, you call us on your cell phone."

"Oh, Daddy, don't fuss. Everything's going to be wonderful."

Staggering into the barn, Faye and Kirsty rolled their eyes at each other.

Robin was already in his old stall. He bumped Faye with his nose as she passed by him.

"Hey, Robbie." She dropped the bags and slipped inside his stall. Robin laid his chin on her shoulder and nuzzled her hair. Faye pressed her cheek against his head. She felt Robin's contentment at being back on the farm.

Outside a pony whinnied. Robin went to the stall door and called back.

"I know," said Faye, "it would be more fun to be out in the field with your buddies, but the princess wants you inside so your hair won't get sun bleached."

"I hope *she's* cleaning his stall," said Kirsty, "because I'm not going to."

Nicole came into the barn. "What are you doing in my pony's stall?"

"Checking his water bucket," muttered Faye.

She squeezed past Robin out of the stall. He bobbed his head. Faye reached out automatically to stroke his long white blaze.

"Excuse me!" Nicole pushed in front of Faye. She held out her hand, palm up, revealing a single sugar cube. "Here you go, Robbie."

The pony gobbled the sugar and bobbed his head for more. "Now, don't be greedy, Robbie. You know you only get one at a time."

Faye bit her lip as Robin nickered to Nicole, begging for another sugar cube. She knew it was only cupboard love but it still hurt to see.

"Our barn has automatic waterers," said Nicole. "Robin never runs out of water in his stall at home. You should get them put in here."

Before Faye could say anything in reply, Riley stuck his head through the opening at the top of the ladder. "Would you girls quit yakking and throw those bags up to me?"

Nicole snatched up a pink knapsack and tossed it wildly into the air. Riley grabbed at it and missed. The knapsack hit the ladder and toppled down onto Faye, knocking her to her knees.

"I'm sorry!" gasped Nicole. "Are you all right?"

Faye stood up, smacking the dust off the knees of her jeans. "I'm okay."

"Nicole, your folks are leaving," Lucy called into the barn. "Come and say goodbye."

"I'll be right back." Nicole trotted off, making kissy noises at Robin as she passed his stall.

Faye and Kirsty watched her go.

"This is going to be one long week," said Kirsty.

"Don't you girls ever stop talking?" asked Riley. He hung over the edge of the loft, arms dangling.

Kirsty pitched a knapsack at him. Riley snagged the nylon handles and slung it into the loft. "Why did she bring so much stuff? Maybe she's moving in...hey, are you two okay?" he asked as Faye and Kirsty clapped their hands to their faces and groaned.

The temperature was climbing by the time all of Nicole's belongings had been lugged up into the hayloft and arranged to her liking.

"It's so hot," said Nicole. "I'm really thirsty. Can I have a drink?"

Faye led the way to the house. In the kitchen she poured everyone a glass of cold water from the tap. Nicole peered into hers. "Don't you have ice?"

Kirsty dug around in the freezer and came up with an empty ice cube tray.

"We always forget to fill it," said Faye.

"That's okay," sighed Nicole. She looked around the cluttered kitchen for a place to sit. Faye gathered up the horse magazines on the table into a stack and lifted an elderly tabby cat off a chair. Kirsty cleared a place for herself and they all sat down.

Faye drained her glass and got up to refill it.

"This water tastes…different," Nicole said as Faye sat down again.

"That's because of the minerals," she explained. "It's from our well."

"Like, from out of the ground?" Nicole eyed her glass uncertainly. "Is it safe to drink?"

Suddenly, Kirsty clutched at her throat. She swayed in her chair, gagging, and tumbled to the floor.

"Oh no! Kirsty, what's wrong?" Nicole rushed to her side.

Faye ducked her head under the table and watched as Kirsty groaned piteously and flailed her limbs.

"She needs help!" Nicole grabbed the phone. "I'm calling an ambulance."

"No!" cried Faye and Kirsty in unison.

Nicole spun around. "Kirsty! You're okay?"

"Of course I am." Kirsty hauled herself back to her chair. "I was just goofing around."

"You were making fun of me!"

"No, I wasn't. It was a joke, Nicole."

"Well, I'm not laughing!" Nicole crossed her arms and slumped down in her chair. "Faye, when are you going to help me?"

"Lucy's giving us a lesson early tomorrow morning when it's cool."

"No, no, I need help from *you*," insisted Nicole.

"Lucy's a great teacher," said Kirsty.

Nicole waved away her words. "She's not the one who rode Robin. Come on, Faye, you've got to tell me. You can even ride Robin. Just give me the secret to getting him to jump."

"Okay, I'll ride him," said Faye.

"Oh, Faye, thank you! This means so much to me. You'll show me tomorrow?"

"Sure, I guess so."

"Promise?"

"I promise."

Nicole slid out of her chair. "Where's the bathroom?"

"Up the stairs. Second door on the left."

As she went upstairs Kirsty leaned across the table. "Now what are you going to do?"

"I'm going to ride Robin tomorrow, just like I promised her."

"What about this riding secret you promised to give her?"

Faye shrugged. "If she wants to believe in some kind of magic secret, that's her problem. All I know is I'm going to ride Robin as much as I can while I've got the chance!"

9

The sun was still just a golden halo behind the mountains early the following morning as they led their saddled ponies into the riding ring. Faye latched the gate behind them and reached for Robin's reins. "I'd better warm him up *and* ride him in the lesson."

"But can't you just show me the secret so I can practise it?" asked Nicole.

"I've got to make sure it still works with him. That might take a while." Faye kept her eyes fixed on Nicole's face, willing her to hand over Robin.

Nicole relinquished the reins. Faye pushed Skylark's into her empty hand. The morning sky suddenly lightened as the sun burst over the mountains.

Swiftly, just in case Nicole changed her mind, Faye lifted the reins over Robin's head, tugged the stirrup irons down the leathers and swung into the saddle. The bay pony tensed, his ears flicking. *Hey, it's me,* she told him silently and felt him let out a long sigh.

Robin felt different than she remembered—smaller somehow. Probably because she was riding in Nicole's saddle instead of her own, Faye decided. Otherwise it was just like old times. All she had to do was think *for-ward* and her partner was off and trotting. They turned and circled, extended and collected. Robin was as supple and responsive as ever. But had his trot always been this bouncy, maybe even choppy? Maybe it was the way Nicole's farrier had trimmed his hooves. She asked him to canter.

It was a perfect moment. Robin rolled along through the soft early morning air, his hooves thumping a steady three-beat rhythm in the sand, Faye rocking gently in the saddle. A faint haze of dust rose in the splinters of sunlight forking through the trees. She tied a bulky knot in the reins to take up the slack and let them go, showing off a little, knowing that with the slightest shift of her shoulders and hips, a second's stiffening of her spine, she could cue the pony to change direction or slow his gait. Robin would do whatever she asked—anything she asked. He trusted her: it was that simple.

Faye felt like bursting into song. If she'd been alone with Robin, just the two of them, she would have. Instead she stretched her cheeks wide in a grin, beaming it like a torch at Kirsty and Nicole, then at Lucy, coming through the gate into the ring, her fingers curled around a mug of coffee. Squinting against the rising sun, she beckoned to Faye.

"Okay, let's switch back ponies and get started," she said. She slipped a pin out of a jump cup and slid the cup down the standard to a lower placing.

"We're trading ponies," Nicole informed her.

"Not today. I've got some exercises I want you to try."

"But I want Faye to ride Robin. She's going to show me...something."

"Nicole, you'll get more out of this lesson on your own pony." Lucy shot her granddaughter a sharp glance. "Come on now, Faye."

Reluctantly, Faye kicked her feet free of the stirrups, slid down from the saddle and led Robin back to Nicole.

"So what is it?" Nicole whispered as they exchanged reins. "What were you doing to make him behave so perfectly?"

Sick with disappointment at having her ride on Robin cut short, Faye could only shrug and shake her head.

"Come on, Faye, I need to know!"

Kirsty edged Lancelot closer. "Nicole, maybe the problem is *you*."

"What do you mean?" Nicole demanded.

"Well, you're so stiff and uptight. You need to relax more, hold the reins looser, like Faye does."

"I'm a good rider! I've got three walls of ribbons at home to prove it," snapped Nicole.

"I didn't mean that," Kirsty protested.

"Oh, what do you know, anyway?" Nicole shoved her boot in the stirrup and flung her leg over Robin. "You made a promise, Faye. You'd better not break it."

"All right, let's get started," called Lucy.

"But I haven't warmed up Lancelot," said Kirsty.

"You and Faye can warm up your ponies while I start with Nicole."

A half-hour later, Kirsty gave Lancelot a long rein, letting him stretch his neck and back. They'd trotted and cantered, circled and serpentined until her pinto was supple and attentive. She cast a sour look at the centre of the ring where Nicole on Robin wound a tight circle around Lucy at the sitting trot, Nicole's arms held straight out from her sides. "I didn't know this was going to be a private lesson," she grumbled as Faye came alongside on Skylark.

Faye watched Robin skip along, his heavy tail swinging gently. Lucy had Nicole drawing big circles in the air with her arms to loosen up her shoulders. Nicole was grinning and giggling at her efforts.

"Nicole always gets her own way."

"It's not fair! Lucy's supposed to be teaching all of us, not just Nicole. Look, she's actually let go of the reins. Big deal," said Kirsty. "I can do that too." She dropped her reins and waved her arms.

"Kirsty, Faye! You two can join us now," said Lucy.

Hastily, Kirsty gathered up her reins. "About time. It's getting hot."

"Over the trot poles," instructed Lucy, gesturing to a line of evenly spaced poles on the ground. Every pole had a jump standard at each end, making a long channel. "Sit tall, heels deep, and remember to look up. Faye, lead off, then Kirsty and Nicole."

As Faye trotted Skylark away she heard Nicole whine, "Do I have to?"

"Yes," Lucy replied curtly, to Faye's satisfaction.

Maybe her grandmother hadn't been totally fooled by Nicole after all.

They went over the trot poles three times: first with both hands on the reins, then one hand and then no hands, guiding the ponies with their legs and bodies. Nicole squealed as Robin high-stepped up the line, extra bounce to his strides as he lifted his legs up to clear the poles.

Lucy pulled them up and began to pin the cups to the jump standards. Faye and Kirsty hopped down and led their ponies over to help. Nicole remained on Robin, twirling her finger around the tip of her blonde pony-tail.

Once the cups were up they placed one end of each rail into them to form a grid of low crosses. "Go ahead," said Lucy when they were done. Faye remounted and began her approach to the crosspoles.

"Now what are we doing?" called Nicole as she passed.

"Same thing."

"Without reins?"

Faye pretended not to hear. Nicole would find out soon enough.

After they'd all been over the line of crosspoles twice, Faye rode over to Lucy. "Should we drop our stirrups?"

"Oh, yes!" said Kirsty. "No stirrups or reins. That's always fun!"

"You mean we're going to jump without our stirrups *or* reins?" said Nicole.

"No reins for sure," said Lucy. "No stirrups is up to you."

Faye had already slid her feet from her stirrups and crossed the leathers in front of her saddle. She tied her reins in a knot so they wouldn't flop about on Skylark's neck. Kirsty shot her a grin and did the same. Nicole knotted her reins. She jammed her boots firmly into her stirrups as if to prevent them from being yanked away.

"Jumping without stirrups is a lot of fun," Faye told her. "Why don't you try it?"

"Come on, Nicole, it's easy. The jumps are really low," urged Kirsty.

"I don't want to."

"Don't worry about falling off. I do all the time and it doesn't hurt. You just slide off over your pony's shoulder." Kirsty demonstrated, hanging over Lancelot's shoulder until she was nearly out of her saddle.

"I'm not worried about falling off!"

Kirsty pulled herself back into position. "Then why won't you try it?"

"What for? We use stirrups in competition so what's the sense of practising without them?"

Faye waited for Lucy to lecture Nicole on the many benefits of working without stirrups, but her grandmother merely sipped her coffee and said, "Why don't you start off, Faye?"

Faye trotted Skylark to the grid and set her eyes on the far side. Hugging the pony's round sides with her legs, arms out from her sides, she dipped and swayed, following the bobbing motion of his body as he hopped over the crosspoles. The trick was to stay squarely in the middle of the pony's back. Skylark, with his broad frame, made it easy. He plunked over the last little jump and trundled around the outside track, guided solely by Faye's legs. She flapped her arms up and down like wings, showing off a little.

By the time she steered Skylark back to the middle of the ring, Kirsty and Lancelot were halfway up the grid. Kirsty had one hand in the mane, off-balanced by her pinto's charging pace over the poles. She shook her head ruefully as they flew over the last jump. "I had to grab mane!"

"That's okay," said Lucy. "Okay, Nicole, it's your go."

"Just a second." Nicole kicked her feet free of the stirrups and laid them across Robin's withers. Squaring her shoulders, she spun the pony around and sent him toward the grid. A stride away from the first crosspole she flung out her arms.

"Good girl," murmured Lucy.

Nicole made it to the third jump before her left hip slid down her saddle flap. She snatched at Robin's mane and pulled herself back into the centre of the seat. Robin kept a true course, bouncing over the crosspoles in a completely straight line.

At the end of the grid Nicole dropped her handhold and grabbed for the reins.

"Very good! Go again, right away," said Lucy.

"It's my turn," Faye protested, but Lucy didn't reply.

After three more trips over the grid, Nicole was securely balanced in the saddle, her legs tight to Robin's sides, her arms out from her sides.

"What's the big fuss all about?" muttered Faye as Lucy heaped praise on Nicole.

"Robin sure looks happier, now that Nicole's not catching him in the mouth with the bit anymore," Kirsty pointed out.

Robin did look more relaxed, soft-eyed and playing gently with his bit as he ambled around Lucy. Nicole patted his neck over and over while Lucy reviewed her performance, smothering the corrections with layers of flattery.

"You'd think she'd just won the gold medal at the Olympics," said Faye.

"Faye and Kirsty, did you notice Nicole's straight back?" called Lucy. "That's what both of you need to work on."

"I took ballet when I was little," said Nicole, walking Robin back to the group. "Andrew says that's why I have such good posture."

Faye, who'd refused as a six-year-old to go back to tap dancing after the first class, scowled and deliberately hunched her shoulders.

"I could teach you some of my ballet exercises. They'd help with your posture. You, too, Kirsty."

"Ballet? No thanks!" Kirsty said. A smile twitched at Faye's mouth. Behind Nicole, Kirsty was striking various ballet-like poses on Lancelot's back.

"Are you sure? Lots of people do ballet—all shapes and sizes. We could trade: ballet exercises for Robin's secret. It sure works, doesn't it? He was so good after you rode him."

Faye gawked at Nicole, amazed she was still hung up on an imaginary secret. Why didn't she realize Robin had improved because she'd ridden him differently?

"Okay, ladies, that's all for today," said Lucy. "You can put your ponies away."

"I'm going to phone my parents right away and tell them how much better Robin's behaving already." Nicole rode the bay pony out the gate behind Lucy.

"Now what are you going to do?" Kirsty asked Faye.

"Nothing. You saw how much Nicole's riding improved after just one lesson with Lucy. By the end of the week she'll be back to normal without any 'secret' from me."

Kirsty smoothed Lancelot's mane. "I hope you're right."

10

"I'm bored," whined Nicole two afternoons later as she lazed in the shade of a lilac bush. "Will you two hurry and get those fence rails fixed so we can do something fun?"

"We're working as fast as we can!" snapped Faye. Her arms and shoulders ached after half an hour of pounding a hammer. Beads of sweat tickled the back of her neck, and under her straw hat her heavy hair pressed against her scalp like a thick woollen blanket. She swung back the hammer in her hand. "Ready, Kirsty?"

Her friend braced the long cedar rail against the fence posts and nodded. "Ready."

Faye took aim at the long nail stuck in one end of the rail and flung her hammer arm forward. The hammer glanced off the nail and hit the rail with such force it bounced out of Kirsty's grip. Both girls groaned.

"Faye, you're useless with that hammer," said Nicole, propping herself up on her elbows. "Why doesn't Riley fix the fences?"

"Because he's working at Arnold's," answered Faye through clenched teeth.

"So why doesn't Lucy hire someone to fix this place up

with all the money my parents paid her for my pony?"

"Because we do things for ourselves on this farm," Faye retorted.

"That's just stupid. This place is a mess. You should pay someone to help you fix it up."

"Just ignore her," Kirsty said under her breath. "Pretend she isn't there."

"I'm trying," muttered Faye, hoisting the rail up, "but it's really hard to do. She's driving me crazy!"

"When's Lucy getting back from grocery shopping?" asked Nicole. "I want to discuss my training program with her."

"Soon," said Kirsty when Faye didn't answer. "She said she'd be home in an hour or so."

Nicole exhaled a long sigh and flopped down into the grass.

"Do you want me to try hammering?" Kirsty asked Faye. "I'm not very good but...Faye? Are you okay?"

Faye blinked slowly. "I feel kind of funny."

"Your face is really red. Maybe we should sit down for a while in the shade."

Faye propped the hammer against the fence. Her arms and legs were trembling, she discovered. Pulling off her hat, she dropped onto the grass and stretched out in the blessed shade. Her ears were filled with the pounding of her own blood, like the crashing of ocean waves on a distant shore. She closed her eyes and felt the cool of the grass beneath her seep into her body.

Gradually the roaring in her ears subsided, so that she

could hear Nicole peppering Kirsty with questions about her lessons with Lucy.

"Faye's helped me a lot, too," Kirsty said.

"She has? What kind of help? Tell me."

"She's been longeing me to improve my position and it really works. My balance is better and my legs are a lot stronger."

"So exactly what does she do?"

"Do you know what a longe line is?"

"Of course I do! It's a long web rope. You attach one end to the pony and make him go around you while you stand in the middle."

"Exactly. Faye makes Lancelot walk and trot while I do exercises and concentrate on improving my position in the saddle."

"Oh, beginner stuff," sniffed Nicole.

"It's not just for beginners. Lucy says longeing is an important part of classical horsemanship. Even Faye gets longed, don't you, Faye?" said Kirsty.

Faye nodded as she propped herself on one elbow and took a long drink from her water bottle.

"Feeling better?" asked Kirsty.

"A lot, except my face is still hot." She pressed the water bottle to her cheek.

"Faye, when are you going to help *me*?" asked Nicole. "Remember, you promised you would."

The throbbing in Faye's skull started up again.

"Don't bother her now, Nicole. Can't you see she doesn't feel well?"

"She said she would help me with Robin. I've only got a few more days before I go home. *When* is she going to do it?"

Faye clenched her jaw. She could not take a single second more of being pestered by Nicole, not another moment. The other girl was like a burr inside her sock, scratching her foot raw every time she moved. She had to do something to get rid of the irritation before she went crazy.

"Right now!" Faye pushed herself to her feet. "Come on, Nicole."

"Hey, where are you going? What's happening?"

"You want me to help you like I help Kirsty? Then get on your riding clothes and come down to the ring."

"All right! Oh, thank you, thank you, Faye." Nicole scrambled to her feet and hurried off.

Faye squared her shoulders and started in the direction of the barn.

Kirsty scooped up the hammer and the coffee can of nails and ran after her. "What are you going to do?" she asked.

"I'm giving Nicole just what she asked for." Faye squinted into the bright sun. "I'm going to teach her a lesson."

"Faye, are you sure you feel okay?" asked Kirsty a short time later, as they led Robin along the path to the riding ring.

"I'm fine."

"But your face is still really red. Maybe you shouldn't do this right now."

"I have to, Kirsty. I promised Nicole. You know that." Faye led the pony through the gate and halted him. "I have to do this."

Kirsty watched her friend anxiously as Faye tightened the girth of Robin's saddle. Except for her flushed cheeks Faye seemed all right, even cheerful. She hummed softly as she unbuckled the stirrup leathers and slipped them off the saddle. There wasn't any visible reason for Kirsty to feel sick to her stomach.

Guess I've been out in the sun too long, like Faye, she thought, and stepped back into a patch of shade.

"Here I am!" Nicole strode into the ring in her breeches and boots, her helmet slung over her arm. She frowned at the stirrupless saddle. "What's going on?"

"You asked me to help you like I help Kirsty, so I'm going to longe you to strengthen your seat and legs and improve your balance." Faye spoke as if she were reciting from a manual of horsemanship.

"But I want you to help me jump Robin!"

"Oh. Well, all right." Faye started to lead Robin back to the gate.

"Where are you going?"

"I'm putting Robin away."

"Okay, okay, you can longe me." Nicole rolled her eyes. "But you still have to help me with Robin's jumping."

"Whatever you want, Nicole," said Faye with a little

smile that stirred the uneasy feeling inside Kirsty again. She clipped the longe line to the cavesson over Robin's bridle and tucked a tall whip under her arm.

Nicole slipped her helmet over her neat blonde ponytail and bent her left leg for Kirsty to boost her into the saddle. "Hey, why are you taking away my reins?"

"You won't be using them. Just rest your hands on your hips." Faye waggled the whip and Robin moved off. She played out the long web rein until he was travelling in a large circle around her. Anchoring one foot to the sand she pivoted on the ball, pushing with her other foot to keep the size of the circle constant.

Perched on the fence, Kirsty studied Nicole's position intently. Even to her untrained eye the other girl looked stiff and awkward in the bare saddle, shoulders hunched and legs clamped against Robin's sides. Used to Faye's easy grace on the back of a pony, Kirsty found it hard to believe that Nicole was also a prize-winning rider.

"So, is this it?" asked Nicole after Robin had made several circles on the end of the long web rein at a slow walk. "Am I done yet?"

"Oh, no, we're just getting started," said Faye. "Are you sure you don't want to try any warm-up exercises?"

"I'm not going to touch my toes or stretch my arms over my head. That's for beginners."

"All right, have it your way," said Faye brightly. "We'll trot now."

She waved the longe whip and Robin sprang into a quick trot. Nicole grabbed the pommel of the saddle.

"Slow him down! How do you expect me to stay on?"

"Relax, Nicole," Faye sang. "Let yourself move with the pony." She shook the whip again. Robin picked up his pace. Nicole bounced higher.

Kirsty felt a flicker of sympathy for her. Sitting to the trot was a tough skill to master. Clinging to the sides and back of a briskly moving pony took balance and muscular strength applied in just the right amount. Too much grip and your legs would give out after a few minutes. Too little and you'd slide right off the pony. You had to learn to let your body go with the pony while keeping your own balance.

Nicole clung to the saddle with both hands. Her face flushed a pale seashell pink. After a few more bone-shaking circuits, the hue deepened to a dark shade of salmon.

"Faye, please stop," Nicole huffed.

"Not just yet!" chirped Faye. She checked her watch. "Not even ten minutes!"

Couldn't Faye see how loose Nicole was in the saddle? Kirsty hopped off the fence and ran over. Out in the sun her forehead prickled instantly with beads of sweat. "She's had enough, Faye. Look, she almost fell off!"

"No, Kirsty, it hasn't been long enough. You go for ten minutes or more." Faye's voice was strangely calm.

"Not at sitting trot! It's really hard work. She's not used to it."

"She should be. *I* can ride at sitting trot for over half an hour."

"Nicole can't. She's not you, Faye."

"She wants to be, doesn't she? She wanted my pony because she wanted to win like me. Well, now she can see just how hard I work." Faye flicked the whip again and Robin trotted harder. "Not everybody has rich parents to buy them trained ponies or hire expensive coaches."

Nicole slumped over, her head flopping with every stride.

"Are you nuts, Faye? Can't you see she can't take any more? You've got to stop!"

Faye shook her head. "Not yet. She needs to do more—what are you doing?"

"Give me that!" Kirsty grabbed the longe line and tried to wrest it away from her. Faye jerked the line away, using her back as a shield.

"Whoa!" screeched Nicole. "Robin, whoa!"

Urged on by the whip waving wildly in Faye's hand, Robin accelerated into gallop.

"Stop it, Kirsty! Let go!" Feeling the line slip through her hands, Faye gave it an almighty yank. Kirsty stumbled forward and fell onto her, knocking them both to the sand. Faye's fingers burned as the line ran through them. Before she could curl them shut they were empty.

Kirsty's elbow dug into her chest and her foot pressed down on her shin as she scrambled to her feet. "Oh no!" She sprinted across the sand.

Spitting sand, Faye rolled onto her knees in time to catch a glimpse of Robin's quarters dodging through the open gate, the longe line fluttering behind him. Above the drumbeat of his hooves she could hear Nicole's wails of terror. Abruptly, all sounds ceased. Pushing herself upright, she ran after Kirsty.

She pounded up the path to the barn to come upon a scene far worse than she could have imagined. Outside the barn doors Robin stood hang-headed, his sides heaving with the longe line trailing in the dirt beside him. Sweat foamed like soapsuds on his shoulders and flanks. She caught her breath as she took in a motionless body sprawled between his splayed feet. Lucy stepped into the picture, quietly backing Robin a few paces and kneeling down beside Nicole.

Faye's feet stalled in their tracks. *Please,* she prayed, *don't let her be...*

Kirsty gathered up the longe line and led the pony off to the side. Lucy spoke softly, her head close to Nicole's. Faye strained to hear a reply. Her grandmother gently ran her hands over Nicole's arms and legs, then rocked back on her heels and held out her hand. Nicole reached up to take it.

Faye swayed, dizzy with relief as Nicole sat up. Seconds later she was standing, swiping at her eyes with the heel of her hand. Lucy helped her pull off her helmet and swatted dust from her shoulders.

"Are you all right?" Faye asked Nicole.

Shrinking back, the other girl glared at Faye over Lucy's shoulder, her bottom lip quivering.

Lucy narrowed her eyes at her granddaughter. "Did you do this?"

"Grandma, I…I'm sorry. I didn't mean—"

"I asked: did you do this? Answer me!"

Faye hung her head. "Yes."

"Kirsty, untack the pony and hose him down. Then walk him until he's dry. Let him have water but not too much at once, no more than six swallows at a time. Come on, Nicole, let's get you to the house and out of this sun."

"I'll help Kirsty," offered Faye, desperate to atone for her behaviour.

"Oh, no, you won't," said her grandmother. "You stay right away from that poor animal. I'll deal with you later."

"Lucy? Grandma, I'm sorry," cried Faye as they shuffled to the house. "Did you hear me? I said I'm sorry!"

Lucy paused, looking back over her shoulder. "I heard you, Faye, but this time being sorry is not enough."

11

"What were you thinking, Faye?" roared Lucy, pacing up and down the tiny living room. "How could you have done that?"

Faye huddled against the arm of the old sofa, trying to hide from her grandmother's fierce glare. She didn't even try to offer answers. There was no defence for what she had done.

"Nicole could have gotten sunstroke, Faye, do you realize that? And Robin—I thought you cared for him. How could you treat him that way?"

Faye felt herself dissolve in shame, tears flooding her eyes. She couldn't stand to be in her own skin. Sick with despair, she ground her face into the arm of the sofa, smearing her tears into the worn fabric.

"Hey, come on, Lucy, you haven't heard Faye's side of the story." Riley leaned in the door.

Their grandmother shook her head. "There's no excuse for abusing an animal like that, none at all!"

A moment later, Faye heard footsteps stomping up the stairs. She lifted her head.

"She's gone to check on Nicole." Riley rolled his eyes to the ceiling.

"Is she…is she okay?" croaked Faye.

"She'll be fine. She had a cool shower and now she's lying down in Grandma's room. Here." He handed Faye a piece of paper towel to blow her nose.

Stubby bounded onto the sofa, worming his sturdy body into her lap. Faye stroked his smooth, bony head, grateful at least one living creature on earth still liked her.

Riley sat beside her and slung his arm around her shoulders, expanding the count to two living creatures. "So what happened, Faye? It's not like you to be cruel to an animal or a person."

Faye crumbled at the kindness in his voice. "I don't understand why I did it! Nicole's got everything and she just keeps bugging me and bugging me and suddenly I just wanted to hurt her like she keeps hurting me. Oh, I'm such a horrible person!"

"No, you're not, Faye." Riley squeezed her shoulders. "You're a good kid—and the best sister in the world. Nicole should never have come here for help. The heck with the farm's reputation and all that crap—it's too much to expect of you."

Faye was startled by the fierce tone of his voice. "Her father's going to sell Robin if he doesn't start winning for Nicole. Then neither of us will see him again!"

"Maybe that would be for the best."

"No!" wailed Faye.

"Okay, okay, I take it back. But you can't keep on like this, Faye."

"What am I supposed to do? I miss Robin so much."

Riley sighed. He hugged her again but offered no answers.

That night Faye went to bed in her own room. She knew Nicole and Kirsty didn't want her around—how could they, after what she'd done?

Nicole had emerged just before supper flushed and subdued. She'd complained about a headache, then had been unusually quiet for the rest of the evening, rocking on the veranda and leafing through horse magazines.

And Kirsty...Faye would never forget the look of disgust on her best friend's face. *Were* they still best friends? Probably not.

Through her open bedroom window she heard Kirsty and Nicole giggling as they made their way to the barn. Faye's eyes ached with tears she could not shed. She was alone, ponyless and friendless, and she had no one to blame but herself. She hung over the side of her bed and dragged out her old, bedraggled stuffed pony from underneath. It was dusty and threadbare, a comforting relic of a time past when she'd been much younger and still a good person. She tucked Pony into her arms and promptly fell asleep.

Sometime in the early hours, she woke in the dark and could not get back to sleep. She squirmed, trying to change position, and found herself wrapped tightly in her sheet like a mummy in a tomb. Panicking, she wriggled free, tossing the sheet to the floor, and sat up.

If only she could fling off her own skin and be some-one other than Faye March.

Through the still night came the rattle of an empty bucket. She leaned out the open window and traced the sound to the barn, where Robin was the lone equine occupant. Perhaps he had drained his bucket dry and needed water. After sweating so hard he'd be extra thirsty.

She jammed her bare feet into the runners lying beside her bed and tiptoed downstairs. Stubby yipped softly as she scurried across the kitchen and slipped out the door. She jumped down the veranda steps and ran into the shadow of the lilac hedge. There she waited until her eyes adjusted to the solid darkness of a country night.

Her feet knew the way to the barn. Robin nickered as she stepped inside his stall.

"Shh, Robbie, don't wake up anyone." She ran her hand along the edge of the stall wall until she came to his water bucket. Her fingers came out wet. The bucket was half full. Another bucket hung beside it, the empty one. Someone—Nicole?—had given the pony two buckets of water to replace the fluids he'd sweated away.

Robin laid his head on her shoulder, nuzzling her hair. Faye felt a relief so keen it stung. "How can you still like me after what I did to you? I didn't mean to hurt you, Robin, I really didn't. I'm so sorry. I don't know what happened to me." A sob burst from her throat. Clinging to Robin, she erupted in a storm of weeping, spilling her tears onto his heavy mane.

"Faye?" A shadowed form hovered at the stall door.

"Who's there?" she gulped, her sobs catching in her throat.

"It's me." Nicole's voice. "What's wrong?"

Faye's heart sank. She wiped her nose on her pyjama sleeve. "Nothing."

The straw rustled as Nicole came into the stall. "What are you doing in here?"

"I...I'll leave." Faye stroked Robin's soft neck one more time and stepped back. Robin bunted her gently.

"Don't go," said Nicole. "I want to talk to you."

"You do?"

"That was a really mean thing you did to me today."

"I know. I'm sorry. Really sorry." It was true; she *was* sorry for the way she'd treated Robin...and Nicole.

"You don't like me, do you?" Nicole asked bluntly.

Faye blurted out the truth. "No!"

"But *why*? What have I ever done to you?" To Faye's astonishment, Nicole sounded genuinely bewildered.

"You took my pony!"

"We *bought* Robin. My dad paid a lot of money for him. And you have so many other ponies. Why are you mad at me for getting Robin?"

"Because Robin's special. He is...he *was*...my partner. We were a team."

Nicole made an impatient sound. "I know he's a special pony but I thought you'd outgrown him. Isn't that why you sold him?"

"Of course not."

"Then why did you?"

"Because we needed the money."

Silence. "So you sold me Robin because you needed the money and now you hate me for buying him. That doesn't make a lot of sense, Faye."

"I'm really sorry," said Faye miserably, "and I don't hate you."

"You do too! You're always laughing behind my back or making fun of me. And I've tried so hard to be friends."

"Nicole…"

"I really thought you were going to help me today. I thought you'd share your secret because you wanted Robin to do well, but instead you…you were just horrible to me and Robin!"

Faye hung her head, truly ashamed.

"So now what, Faye?"

"What do you mean?" she asked.

"I can't go home for another three days, when my parents are back. What's going to happen until then? Do you have more tricks planned for me?"

"Oh, no, Nicole. I promise."

Nicole sniffed. "Lot of good your promises are."

"I mean it, Nicole. Things will be different."

There was a long silence. Nicole's voice, when she spoke, sounded thin and far away. "It used to be so easy, every time I went in a class at a horse show I'd win. But something happened—I don't know what. I started having problems with my ponies. They'd run out or stop or hit rails. It seemed the harder I worked at my riding the worse things got.

"Then there was Robin. He always jumped—always! No matter what happened he'd go. Remember that class, Faye, when you lost your stirrups *and* your reins and you still won the championship?"

"Yes." How could Faye forget? It had been her last horse show with Robin.

"He was amazing. I knew if he were mine I could go to all the big shows and not have to worry. Except it's not turning out that way."

"Let me have him back, Nicole, please. I'll get the money somehow. If he's not working out for you—"

"Why would you want him back the way he's jumping? Unless you know how to get him to jump, something you're not telling me."

"I keep telling you: I have no secret way of riding Robin," said Faye.

"I don't believe you," said Nicole. "I just can't believe you."

The straw rustled and a moment later the door creaked.

"Nicole?" No answer. Faye was alone with Robin. "Now what happens?" she asked the pony.

There was a half beat of silence; then Robin resumed chewing. Faye leaned on his shoulder and listened to his strong teeth steadily grind each mouthful of hay in a rhythm as familiar as her own heartbeat.

12

"Faye?"

Hunkered down in front of the barn scrubbing water buckets, Faye looked up to see Kirsty holding Lancelot by the reins. "Sorry," she mumbled and scooted over to make room for them to leave the barn.

"Aren't you riding with us this morning?"

Faye shook her head.

"Oh." Kirsty didn't sound surprised.

Why would she? thought Faye morosely. Of course Lucy would ban Faye from riding after yesterday afternoon's disaster.

"I'm sorry," her friend said.

"Me too."

"I guess I should get over to the ring."

"Probably. Lucy will be out any minute."

"Well, see you later." Kirsty led her pony along the path to the riding ring.

Faye wielded her scrub brush with renewed vigour, a sliver of hope wriggling through her gloom. At least her best friend was speaking to her again.

"What's going on?" asked Lucy, coming around the

corner of the barn.

Faye pushed a tangle of hair out of her eyes and got up. She waved the scrub brush at the row of clean buckets. "I didn't know what you wanted me to do this morning—"

"Why aren't you ready to ride?"

"Ride?"

"Yes, Faye, ride. In the lesson with Kirsty and Nicole."

"I didn't think I was allowed to…after yesterday."

Lucy's sharp green eyes drilled into her. "Hmm. Well, Nicole explained everything."

"She did? What did she say?" The scrub brush fell from Faye's fingers.

"She told me she asked you to longe her on Robin the way I longe you. I'm still really disappointed in you, Faye. You know better than to work a pony and rider so hard in this heat!"

"I know, Grandma. I'm really sorry."

"Well, Nicole and Robin both seem okay today, thank goodness. But think next time, Faye. Don't let yourself be pushed into doing the wrong thing!"

"I won't," vowed Faye.

"Now hurry up and get ready. It's going to be another scorcher today. Let's get riding before it's too hot. Where are the other two?"

"Kirsty's already in the ring with Lancelot. Nicole *was* here a few minutes ago." Faye squinted into the barn. Robin stood tied in the alley, saddled but not bridled.

"Find her and tell her to get a move on, will you?"

Hurrying into the barn Faye heard footsteps above in the hayloft. She started up the ladder.

"Daddy! Why didn't you tell me?" Nicole's voice rang out through the opening above.

Faye climbed to the top of the ladder and peeked into the loft. Nicole sat on her hay bale bed, her cell phone pressed to her ear.

"Yes, he's much better. It's just that it's a really big show, Dad. You should have told me before you entered us in it!"

She stood up. Faye pulled back. "Yes, I'm training really hard...well, not very high, maybe three feet. But Lucy says it's not the height of the jumps that's important in training; it's *how* you jump. We've been doing all kinds of fun exercises, like jumping without stirrups or reins—" Abruptly, she broke off.

A few seconds of silence passed. "No, no, Dad, please don't phone Lucy. I'll tell her to put the jumps higher. I've got to go now. Love you too. Bye."

Faye ducked as Nicole threw down the cell phone and stomped across the loft. She frowned at Faye perched on the ladder. "Were you eavesdropping on my private conversation?"

"Oh, no! Lucy asked me to find you. And...I want to thank you."

"For what?"

"For explaining to Lucy about what happened yesterday. That was nice of you."

"Whatever. So what does Lucy want?"

"You're late for the lesson."

Nicole shrugged. "I had an important phone call."

"Well, you'd better hurry. Lucy might have to cut our lesson short if it gets too hot."

"She'd better not," warned Nicole. "My parents are paying good money for these lessons."

Faye blinked. It hadn't occurred to her that the Walshes might be paying Lucy to help Nicole with Robin.

"I can't get down with you in the way," said Nicole.

Faye scrambled down the ladder and, scooping up a halter, ran out to the pasture to catch Sparrow.

"Look at her fly!" said Kirsty as Nicole and Robin leaped the coop and galloped along the far side of the ring. "She's like a completely different rider."

Faye nodded, watching Nicole rein Robin down to a walk. The other girl was grinning, her cheeks flushed as she patted the pony on the neck. Kirsty was right. Relaxed and confident, Nicole was definitely not the same rider they'd seen at the Valleyview show less than a week ago. It seemed like magic.

"All right, let's put the fences up!" said Lucy. Faye and Kirsty kicked their feet free of their stirrups and, sliding down from their ponies, got to work.

Minutes later, Faye hoisted the last pole in its cup. She stepped back to survey the raised course. Beside her Kirsty clapped her hands to her face. "These jumps are too big!" she wailed. "I can't jump this high."

"You don't have to," said Lucy, overhearing. "This course is for Nicole. She's got an important horse show next weekend and needs to practise over bigger fences."

"Oh, thank you! I was really scared there for a bit. Those jumps are enormous!"

Looking over Kirsty's shoulder, Faye saw Nicole's eyes grow large in her narrow face. Her neck sank into her shoulders like a turtle's.

"Nicole, ride these the same way you did the lower fences," said Lucy. "Don't do anything different. Okay, you can start."

Nicole nodded grimly. She circled Robin once, twice and then a third time before turning to the first jump.

"Come on now, more pace," called Lucy. She clapped her hands in a steady rhythm to encourage Nicole to ride with energy.

Robin loped up to the fence and in slow motion heaved over it. He landed and broke to trot.

Lucy cupped her hands around her mouth. "Get a move on, Nicole!"

Nicole sat frozen in the saddle, feet jammed stiffly into the stirrups, arms rigid at her sides. Robin jogged to the next jump, rocked back on his hocks and pogo-sticked into the air, jolting his rider onto his neck.

"Pull up!" Lucy beckoned Nicole over. "Look, don't change your riding because the fences are higher—"

"I'm not!" protested Nicole. "I'm riding just the same as I did before."

"It's natural to be a little nervous about jumping big

fences. Take a few breaths to relax—"

"I'm not nervous about the height!"

Faye and Kirsty looked at each other.

"Okay, give it another try. Go faster this time," said Lucy.

Nicole urged the pony into his usual bouncy canter. As they came into the jump, her back and arms stiffened, shortening Robin's stride until he was practically hopping on the spot. His hindquarters dipped for takeoff and then, abruptly, he propped his front legs and slid to a stop.

"This is what he always does!" howled Nicole.

"Let's try again," said Lucy mildly.

This time Robin refused the jump two strides out. Nicole burst into tears. "Why won't Faye help me?"

Lucy's face was unreadable as she went over to Nicole and spoke softly. Swiping at her nose, Nicole kicked her feet out of the stirrups and slid off Robin's back.

"Is Lucy letting her give up?" asked Kirsty in amazement as Nicole led Robin into the centre of the ring.

"I don't—" Faye broke off as Nicole came up beside her and grasped Sparrow's reins. Lucy gestured to Robin's empty saddle. "Hop on and take him around."

Faye vaulted down off Sparrow. She took Robin's reins from Nicole and slid her foot into the stirrup. She glanced back to make sure this was what Lucy really wanted.

"Come on, get on," urged Lucy.

Faye swung her leg over Robin and settled into the saddle. She wiggled in the cushioned seat to find her balance and took up contact with the reins. Softly squeezing her legs against the pony, she asked him to canter.

A moment of tension; then Robin relaxed into his rolling canter. Faye circled and sent him to the jumps. She hugged her legs tightly against his barrel and ratcheted up the speed. Robin jumped best at a quick pace, using his momentum to help him fly over the fences.

After one or two sticky jumps Robin bounded over the entire course as if he had springs in his hooves. It was so easy, Faye thought as they sailed over the last fence. Now Nicole had to admit all their jumping problems were completely her fault.

Faye patted the pony's neck as she slowed him down. She took him back to Nicole.

"Thank you," Nicole said stiffly as Faye slid to the ground.

"All right, Nicole, let's give it another try," said Lucy. "A couple of deep breaths to stay soft and relaxed and—"

"Oh, I won't have any problems now," said Nicole. "He's always good after Faye rides him."

She was right. Robin jumped around the course as easily as if the big jumps were crosspoles, Nicole at complete ease in his saddle.

"What are we going to do, Grandma?" whispered Faye. "She believes I have some kind of secret charm."

Lucy shook her head. "There's nothing more we can do. What Nicole needs she has to find in here." Lucy tapped one finger to her chest, just below the left side of her collarbone.

13

The jumps stayed up for Nicole's next three lessons on the farm.

She and Robin soared over fence after fence in such perfect harmony that Faye began to believe Nicole's problems were fixed. She didn't even need Faye to ride Robin first. Faye's last shred of hope, the daydream of Nicole in a fit of pique and frustration simply giving Robin back, faded away. He was gone for good, she realized sadly. She forced herself to try to be happy for Robin. The bay pony sparkled with good care and contentment. He pranced his way out to the ring each morning, looking forward joyfully to jumping now that his rider wasn't hindering his performance.

Faye noted his shining black eyes and eagerly pricked ears with a sharp stab of jealousy that she struggled to smother. She had to accept that Robin had a new rider; that he wasn't coming back to her; that now she had... nothing.

Skylark was sold, and Sparrow was talented but young and inexperienced. Faye had brought along many green ponies. She knew it would be months of practice over simple courses and low jumps in local schooling shows to build his confidence before his courage and ability could be tested over higher fences in more serious competitions. For now, she had no pony to compete with at the upper levels of jumping.

Competition isn't everything, she reminded herself sternly. *Be grateful for what you do have. Look at Kirsty; she's never ridden in a horse show in her life. She's happy just to have a pony and be riding.*

Faye couldn't help it, though. She really missed the challenges of competing over big jumps. She tried hard not to think of the summer ticking by and all the important horse shows she was missing. Without top-level competition to keep her sharp, would she lose her edge, the instant responses that had made her a winning rider? How would she keep her "eye," her perfect ability to judge the striding to a jump, over such small fences? At night, when she ran through her dream of riding in international competition, she was dismayed to find the colour fading, just a little.

Then it was time for Nicole and Robin to leave.

The morning of the departure Faye and Kirsty helped Nicole pack up her things. During the week her belongings had taken on a life of their own and strewn themselves about the entire barn.

"How many different kinds of shampoo did you bring?" asked Faye, on her hands and knees fishing a half-empty plastic bottle out from behind a bale of hay.

"Only three. I have problem hair," explained Nicole. "And that's conditioner, not shampoo."

Faye read the label. "For flyaway hair. Does it work?"

"Oh, yes!" She eyed Faye's unruly curls. "You can keep it if you want."

"Thanks." Faye tucked the bottle to one side to retrieve later. She rocked back on her heels and surveyed the hayloft. "I think we've got everything."

Nicole looked at her watch. "My parents are late as usual."

Kirsty stuck her head into the loft. "Anything else left to go?"

"Looks like that's all," Faye told her.

"Oh, Kirsty, could you do something for me?" asked Nicole. "I'm missing a pair of boot socks. I think Lucy might have mixed them up with Faye's laundry."

"Uh-oh. You'll never find them again if they were put in Faye's room," warned Kirsty, "but I'll go to the house and ask Lucy."

It was already stifling hot in the loft. Faye crawled over the bales to the big window under the eaves. She shimmied onto the sill and dangled her legs over the edge.

"Careful, Faye, don't fall," cautioned Nicole.

Faye rolled her eyes. She'd been sitting like this for years. It was a great place to see out over the farm.

To her surprise, Nicole squeezed in beside her. Clutching the frame, she gazed down at the barnyard below. "Ooh, it's a long way down."

"It sure is," agreed Faye. "Probably break every bone in your body if you fell."

Nicole edged backwards.

A trickle of a cool breeze wafted through the heavy air. Faye sniffed, certain she could smell sap from the poplar trees. On cue a dark cloud scudded out from behind the mountains and raced across the sky. "Oh, thank goodness, it's finally going to rain," she said. "Let's hope we get a good soaking. The pastures really need it."

"My stuff will get wet!" Nicole peered down at the pile of suitcases and knapsacks beside the barn.

"Better move it, then," said Faye. She started to get up. "I'll help you."

"No, wait." Nicole pulled her back down. "I've got to talk to you. Look, I know we aren't exactly friends, but I need you to do something for me."

"What?" asked Faye warily.

"My dad's entered me in the River Valley Horse Show next weekend. If Robin doesn't win the Junior derby, he'll sell him."

"You've got a chance," said Faye curtly. She didn't want to think about Robin competing in a big show like River Valley without her.

"A chance isn't good enough! He's serious, Faye; he's emailed pictures to a trainer in California. Robin has to win! I can't lose him now, not when things are starting to work out between us. He's special, just like you said. Sometimes when I'm riding him I get this feeling we can do anything together!"

"So what do you have to worry about?"

"I don't get that feeling all the time, not yet. What if I don't have it at the horse show? Robin might lose…and

I'll lose him."

"What do you want from me?" Faye waited for Nicole to plead for a magic secret.

"I want *you* to ride him in the show."

"What? That doesn't make sense. Your parents bought Robin for you to ride, not me."

"That's why I want you to pretend to be me."

"You want me to jump Robin in the River Valley Horse Show and somehow fool everyone into believing it's you? That's the craziest thing I ever heard. It would never work!"

"It would," insisted Nicole. "I know it would."

Faye blinked at her in disbelief. "Nicole, we don't look anything alike!"

"*Everyone* looks the same in a riding jacket and helmet. Only our faces will show. We've both got pale skin and we can wear sunglasses."

"And what about this?" Faye twisted a curl of her bright red hair around her finger.

"We'll tuck your hair up under your helmet."

"We'd never get away with it!"

"Yes, we would! Listen, I've got it all worked out. Here's how we'll do it. I've got two riding jackets that are just about the same. You'll wear one of them and wait in the stands, near the in-gate. I'll warm Robin up and then, just before he goes into the ring, you'll get on. Then, at the end of the course, we'll change back again. Simple, right?"

"No! It's the nuttiest idea I've ever heard!"

"I can't think of anything else and I've got to do something!"

"Nicole, even if I did ride Robin in the horse show there's no guarantee I'd win."

"But you would. You always win with Robin."

Faye thumped her head against the frame. "And how would me winning help *you*? I can't ride Robin for you in every horse show."

"It'll give me more time to work on things with Robin. The last couple of days things have really gotten better."

"Well, you've got nearly a week until the show."

"Not enough time. I need more."

"Can't you just tell your dad that?"

Nicole shook her head. "I've tried! He won't listen. He thinks a pony is like a machine and all you do is get on and ride. Faye, please help me. You're my only hope."

In the barnyard below, Stubby erupted into a fit of barking. Faye turned away from Nicole's pleading face to see a dark blue truck and a white horse trailer rolling up the driveway. Mr. and Mrs. Walsh had finally arrived.

"I can't, Nicole. I don't want to get into any more trouble."

"You won't! I promise. If anything goes wrong I'll take all the blame."

Kirsty came out of the farmhouse empty-handed.

"She didn't find your socks," said Faye.

"I've got all my socks. That was an excuse so I could talk to you alone," said Nicole.

Ken Walsh flagged down Kirsty. He turned around,

his gaze following her arm as she lifted it in the air to point at Faye and Nicole in the hayloft, sitting side by side.

"Tell me one thing: why should I do this for you?" asked Faye.

The look in Nicole's eyes was shrewd. "Because you miss that special feeling you had with Robin, don't you?"

Faye nodded slowly, remembering. When she was astride her old partner, nothing could stand in their way. All she had to do was ask and Robin would use every muscle in his body to clear the jumps before them. Teamed up, they made a total far greater than the sum of their two parts.

"I'm giving you a chance to feel it one more time," Nicole went on. "Will you do it, Faye? Will you ride Robin in the River Valley Horse Show?"

"Yes. I'll do it." Already Faye could see herself on Robin, leaping over gleaming fences scattered on a bright green carpet of grass. A derby course! Not only the usual rail and plank fences but banks and ditches and grobs, maybe even a water jump.

"All right!" Nicole clambered to her feet. "I'll get my parents to arrange everything. We'll call you in a few days."

"Wait a moment. I've got one condition: Kirsty comes to the show, too."

"Okay, but you can't tell her anything. Promise you'll keep our plan secret?"

Faye nodded. "I promise."

14

When four days passed without any word from the Walshes, Faye began to suspect Nicole had given up on her crazy scheme. She wasn't sure whether she felt more relieved or disappointed.

Early the next morning a phone call from Mr. Walsh set everything into motion. Just a day later Faye found herself gliding along the highway tucked between Nicole and Kirsty in the back seat of the truck, with Robin in the trailer behind, over the Coast Mountains into the wide, green Fraser Valley. Mr. Walsh turned off the busy highway and tensely navigated the big rig through crowded side streets until they pulled into the showgrounds.

Faye leaned across Kirsty to see out the window. The River Valley grounds looked like any other showgrounds, but even through the thick glass she could feel the excitement in the air. The truck and trailer pulled into the stable area allotted to Andrew's students, and Robin was unloaded and handed over to the grooms.

"I can look after him," said Faye.

Mr. Walsh shook his head. "The grooms know what to do. We have to check in at the hotel."

"You're our guests, dear," added Nicole's mother.

Dazed, Faye was swept off along with Kirsty and Nicole to swim in the hotel pool, dine in a restaurant with white tablecloths and sleep in a soundless room with carpeting so thick it practically covered her bare toes when she walked on it. When she and Lucy went to an overnight show they camped out, usually in the back of the horse trailer, although lately Lucy had talked about buying a second-hand camper for the truck. They cooked their meals on a camp stove and went swimming at the local recreation centre.

Early the next morning a groggy Mr. Walsh ferried them back through nearly deserted streets to the showgrounds for the course walk, steering the truck one-handed while he sipped coffee.

"Come on," Nicole said, running off in the direction of the jumper ring. Kirsty stumbled along, but Faye followed slowly, soaking up the familiar sights and sounds of a horse show, her spirits lifting with every step.

Reaching the ring Faye placed a foot down on the springy green turf and shivered. The densely packed grass felt solid and real under the sole of her boot. She wasn't dreaming as she'd done so many times. She was truly here in the jumper ring under a cloud-quilted sky at River Valley.

"Are you cold, too?" asked Kirsty, huddling inside her jacket against the damp coastal air.

"No, I'm just...excited!"

Kirsty rubbed at her sleep-puffy eyes. "What can you

be excited about so early in the morning?"

Faye caught herself just in time. She'd promised Nicole not to tell anyone about their plan—*Nicole's* plan—to trade places, and that included Kirsty. "Oh, just being at a big horse show," she answered truthfully.

Kirsty would probably think she was nuts to go along with Nicole's scheme and try to talk her out of her part in it.

It *was* a crazy plan. Faye admitted that to herself every time she thought about it. So she didn't. Instead she focused on jumping Robin again, replaying memories of past triumphs over and over.

Now she cleared her mind of everything except the jump course before her. She surveyed the broad, rolling expanse of grass littered with fences of every kind, their crayon-bright colours muted in the pearly light. As far as she could tell from this viewpoint, the widely varied jumps had one thing in common: they were all big. A thrill of anticipation tickled her spine.

Beside her Kirsty yawned. "I could have slept in at the hotel and come with Mrs. Walsh, you know."

"Come on, grumpy." Faye caught Kirsty by the sleeve and pulled her along. "Look, the others are already at the first jump. We have to catch up."

Andrew Baumgartner stood with Nicole and three other students before the jump, studying it intently. Nicole nibbled on her thumbnail while Andrew demonstrated the correct approach to the wide oxer with its red and white barber-striped poles. "Good morning," he said as Faye and Kirsty approached.

"These are my friends Faye March and Kirsty Hagen. I asked them to walk the course with me," explained Nicole.

"Oh, hi, Faye. I didn't recognize you out of riding clothes. What classes are you riding in?"

"I'm not entered in the show," said Faye.

"Oh! So you're here to cheer on Nicole. Well, that's good of you. We all need a cheering section from time to time. Now, has anybody learned the jump-off?"

"I have!" A girl in flannel pyjama bottoms and a polar fleece recited a sequence of numbers. Out of habit Faye repeated them as they were called out, adding a simple tune to make a jingle that would be easy to recall.

"Excellent, Jill, glad to see you're wide awake. Has anybody seen Curtis? No? Where *is* that young man?" The coach looked around for the elusive Curtis. "Well, he'll just have to walk the course by himself. Okay, on to the second fence."

As Andrew strode off, Nicole clutched Faye's arm, pinning her in front of the oxer. "Look how big it is— and it's only the first fence!"

Faye gave the jump a long, hard look. The oxer had to be maximum height and width. It did seem to be a very imposing obstacle for the first jump of the course. She'd have to be sure to bring Robin in at a brisk pace.

They scurried to the next fence. Earnestly waving his arms, Andrew gave detailed instructions on how to ride it. His voice receded to background noise. Faye walked a direct line to the obstacle, keeping her eyes fixed on the top rail, imagining her approach—a pair of tiny curved ears framing the jump as it came closer and closer, dropping lower in her field of vision with every stride until they were airborne.

"Okay, people, let's move on," said Andrew, breaking into a jog.

"It's huge!" someone gasped as they came up to the third obstacle. The students stood back from the triple bar, chattering shrilly. Faye's stomach gave a little lurch. Silhouetted against the wide expanse of grey sky, the jump seemed enormous.

"The jump crew must have made a mistake, Andrew," said Nicole. "Tell the course designer to measure it. This jump's got to be over-height."

"Look, everyone." Andrew stood beside the triple bar and measured the top pole against his ribcage. "See, it's okay. Maybe even an inch under the maximum height."

"It sure looks a lot higher," grumbled one of the other students.

"That's because it's on a slope. Once you get to the top it's lower." Andrew demonstrated, striding up the rise. "Come on, see for yourselves."

The group trudged up the slope.

"I feel sick to my stomach," the girl in pyjamas confided to Faye. "How about you?"

"I can't wait to ride it," said Faye eagerly. "I mean, one day. This course would be a lot of fun *if* I were riding."

The girl grunted, too absorbed in her own nervousness to pay attention to Faye's babbling.

Faye moved to the fringes of the little group to avoid making the mistake of talking to anyone again.

The fourth fence was a stone wall with a pair of rustic rails on top, solid and straightforward. Andrew herded them past with a dismissive wave of his hand.

"Come at it boldly. Keep up your pace; it's a long gallop around these other jumps to number five." He led the way around a cluster of tightly spaced jumps.

The others went on but Faye held back, studying the placement of the jumps. Years of competing on ponies against longer-strided horses had taught her to take the short route between jumps to make up time. If she angled Robin in the air over the wall, they could land to the left. Then they could turn sharply and find a path inside the cluster of jumps, saving at least eight or nine strides and a significant amount of time.

Faye traced out the track. It was tight but it could be done.

"No, no, take the outside line!" shouted Andrew.

Startled, Faye whirled around to find Nicole was following in her footsteps.

"This way saves a lot of strides," Nicole protested.

Andrew scowled. "*Not* a good idea! What if you miss the turn?"

"Then I'll go outside."

"Or collide with another jump. No, Nicole, it's too risky. Come and walk this line."

"But going all the way around will take more time,"

grumbled Nicole. "Taking the inside turn is the way to win the jump-off, isn't that right, Faye?"

Faye nodded, startled that Nicole had figured out the same strategy. She shouldn't have been, though. Nicole had won many jump-offs in the past.

"We have to go clear in the first round to make it into the jump-off," Faye reminded her.

"You will," said Nicole. "You have to."

"We're all waiting for you, Nicole and Faye," called Andrew. "Hurry up, please!"

The next fence was the liverpool. They gathered around and solemnly stared down at the shallow water-filled trough under a single pole.

"No problem for your pony, Nicole," said Andrew. "Just keep your eyes up and use a lot of leg."

The group fell quiet as they walked the rest of the course, subdued by the challenges each jump offered.

"So what do you think?" asked Nicole as they walked to the final jump—a huge green coop topped with a white rail.

Faye started to say the course looked like a lot of fun, and stopped. If she made it sound too easy Nicole might change her mind and ride Robin in the derby herself.

"It's a tough course," said Faye, shaking her head, "really tough. Robin doesn't like ditches and there are two really wide ones."

Nicole pulled Faye close. "You'll try to win, won't you?"

Faye looked her in the eye. "I'll do my very best."

Ken Walsh joined them at the end of the course, a Styrofoam cup of coffee steaming in each hand.

"Morning, Andrew!" he boomed, handing him a cup. "Well, Nicole, have you got your winning strategy all figured out?"

Nicole cringed. "Daddy, shh! You're embarrassing me."

"Embarrassed? What for?"

"Because I might not win, that's why," she hissed.

"Of course you're going to win! You told me you'd fixed all your problems with that pony."

"I have, Daddy, but there are lots of other good riders here."

"Nicole, you *are* the best. Say it: I *am* the best."

"Daddy, please," implored Nicole.

"Come on, honey, say it!"

"I am the best," she muttered, eyes rolling.

"That's my girl! Now *believe* it."

"Excuse me, Ken, but I'm trying to finish up here," interrupted Andrew. "All right, people, any questions about the course?"

"What do you think of those jumps?" asked Kirsty as they wandered back to the stables after the course walk. Nicole had been pulled aside by her parents for a pep talk with Andrew.

"Huh?" Faye had been lost in thought, imagining riding Robin over the derby course.

"The jumps," Kirsty repeated. "They're awfully big."

"Robin can handle them. As long as I—as long as Nicole keeps the pace up he'll have no problem."

They turned down the shedrow where all of Andrew's students had their horses and ponies stabled. Faye admired the burgundy and green banner running along the top of the stalls and the matching tack trunks neatly positioned beside the doors.

One day I'll have all this, she decided. *One day when I'm a professional rider.* Her determination to climb to the top of the ranks burned through her anew. She *would* do it, somehow, someday.

The clopping of horse hooves tugged her away from her reverie. She turned to look as an elderly man came around the far end of the shedrow with a gleaming black mare. The horse stopped suddenly, slender ears snapping forward. She fluted her nostrils, scenting the air, her dark-eyed gaze fixed on Faye.

A frisson ran along Faye's spine. Her feet moved toward the mare. She was certain she'd never seen this horse before—she would never have forgotten such a magnificent creature—but she felt a connection to her.

"Girls, do you know where Curtis is?" asked the old man. "He was supposed to be here fifteen minutes ago to exercise my horse." He tipped his head to the mare, bowing to royalty.

"I'm sorry, I don't know who Curtis is," said Faye.

"Aren't you girls students of Andrew Baumgartner's?"

"No, but we're helping a friend who is. Nicole Walsh. We just finished walking the course with her."

"Hey, I just remembered something," said Kirsty. "At the beginning of the walk Andrew asked where Curtis was and no one knew."

"That's right," said Faye. "No one's seen him yet this morning."

The man clicked his tongue in dismay. "So now he's missed walking the course. That boy! Where could he be?"

The mare stretched her neck, blowing gently on Faye's cheeks. "What's her name?"

"This is Elan. Andrew, there you are! Curtis is late and no one seems to know where he is."

Andrew bustled along the shedrow toward them. "Just got a call from his mother, Laurence. Bad news, I'm afraid. Curtis has fallen off his skateboard, maybe broken his wrist. They're taking him for X-rays."

"What on earth was he doing on his skateboard the morning of a horse show?"

Andrew shrugged helplessly.

"This is a real mess. We've been training Elan for months for this show and now she has no rider!"

"Well, Laurence, I've got a suggestion." The trainer turned to Faye. "How'd you like to ride Mr. Devries' horse?"

"Me? Do you really mean it?"

"Whoa there a moment, Andrew. Just who is this young lady?" asked Mr. Devries.

"Laurence, this is Faye March. She's been riding since she was born. Her grandmother raises the famous Hillcroft ponies, so Faye's had a lot of experience with youngsters. I can't think of anyone better to ride your mare. It's just luck she's here at the show."

Mr. Devries gave Faye a hard look from beneath his bushy eyebrows. She stiffened her backbone and tried not to squirm under his flinty gaze.

"I don't know, Andrew. She's very young," said Laurence Devries finally.

Faye bit her lip to contain her disappointment.

"But if you say she's a good rider, I'll try her on Elan. She can exercise her in the warm-up ring. We'll see how that goes and take it from there."

"Good, good. Okay, Faye, let's fix you up with some boots and a helmet," said Andrew.

"I've got my stuff in the tack room," said Faye without thinking. She winced; would the coach wonder why she'd brought her riding gear to a show when she wasn't supposed to be riding?

Andrew's mind was full of other details. He dug out his cell phone. "Excellent! Hurry and get ready and I'll give your grandmother a call."

"Oh, but I have to see if Nicole needs me," said Faye, belatedly remembering the reason she was at River Valley. "I'm supposed to be helping her."

"Don't worry, I'll explain everything to Nicole and her parents," said Andrew. "Come on, Laurence, let's get Elan tacked up."

"Faye, I can't believe this is happening," said Kirsty as they ducked into the curtained stall being used as a change room. "Elan is the most beautiful horse I've ever seen! And now you're going to ride her. It's like a fairy tale come true. You must be so excited!"

Digging her breeches out of the knapsack she'd stowed in the corner, Faye nodded wordlessly. Her heart was thumping, her teeth chattering if she didn't clamp them tightly together. Everything was happening so quickly. She pulled on the snug cotton stretch pants and unzipped her boot bag.

"Good thing you've got all your stuff...Faye, aren't those your show clothes?"

"Uh-huh." Faye was fumbling with her second boot's hooks, trying to slip them into the nylon loops inside her boot tops.

"Why did you bring them?"

"Well..." Faye hesitated, wanting badly to share the plan with Kirsty. It didn't feel right to keep such a big secret from her best friend, but she'd promised Nicole. "Just in case," she finished lamely. She managed to hook both loops and slid her foot into the tall boot. Standing up, she stamped her heel down into the boot.

"Well, it's a good thing you did," said Kirsty. She passed Faye her helmet.

Raking her fingers through her bushy red hair, Faye bound it into a snug ponytail and tucked the end under. She settled her helmet on top and fastened the clasp. "Okay, let's do this." She paused at the door curtain to take a deep breath. *Take it easy,* she told herself. *You're just going to ride a horse.* Her butterflies refused to settle down. She parted the curtain still feeling she was about to have the biggest audition of her life.

A saddled and bridled Elan fidgeted outside the tack room, her owner holding the reins.

"Hey, pretty mare." Without hesitation, Faye rubbed her palm over the tiny star on the horse's forehead, right between the shining black eyes. Elan tensed, as if to toss Faye's hand away, then submitted to the caress.

"Up you go." Andrew boosted Faye into the saddle and the world narrowed to a pair of slender black ears flicking restlessly and a long, gleaming neck. Looking down, she could see the peak of Andrew's cap; she was sitting higher than she'd ever ridden before.

She draped her legs along the mare's barrel, finding the long swell of her ribs, and slipped her boots into the irons. Elan minced off, stiff-necked, her eyes rolling back to check out the new rider in her saddle. Faye softened all the muscles in her lower spine and felt the mare's tension ease a fraction. She gathered up the reins to the softest of contacts, as if each thin leather strip were made of silken thread. She pulled in a deep breath and exhaled slowly. Elan mimicked her, letting out her breath in a long sigh that stretched her long neck.

Faye guided her supercharged mount out of the stable area to the exercise ring. Andrew, Kirsty and Laurence Devries trailed in their wake. Unnoticed she jigged past Nicole and her parents, looking down at the tops of their heads from her vantage point astride Elan. The mare was a coiled spring of power contained only by the leather reins in Faye's hands and her legs wrapped against the barrel. A quiver she couldn't quite identify zinged through Faye. Fear? Excitement? Or a bit of both?

Glancing back she caught Mr. Devries' stern gaze upon her. Instantly Faye was aware of her slumped shoulders. She pulled them back and checked her position in the saddle against a mental list. Head up, heels down, elbows relaxed. She rode into the exercise ring crowded with horses and riders, and there was no more time to consider anything but how to keep Elan under control.

The constantly questing thin ears heard everything: the thump of a pole falling to the sand, a rider's growl at his lazy mount, a Jack Russell terrier yapping at a low-flying gull. Another horse passed close by and Elan shot sideways, tail lashing like an angry cat's, nearly ducking out from under Faye.

"Sorry," called the rider, but Faye barely heard the apology. She knew nothing beyond the black mare, the mane ruffling on the snaky neck, the dip and sway of the sturdy body under her. It was like riding the crest of a wave, rolling and lifting and floating. She had to fit herself into that energy, become part of the grace and strength.

She felt the mare settling, her mind calming, attention turning to her rider. Faye thought *canter* and they were rolling over the sand, so smoothly it was a surprise to realize they were flying past all the others. Absolute joy fizzed inside Faye. She felt like bursting into song and contented herself with loud humming.

"Faye!" Andrew was beckoning from the centre, pointing to a low jump between him and Mr. Devries. "Bring her in at a trot."

She steadied Elan down to the slower gait and turned off the rail to the jump. Five strides out the mare spotted the obstacle in her path. She tore the reins through Faye's grasp and shot forward. The sudden rush rocked Faye onto the back of the saddle. Before she could get with the motion, Elan was flying over the jump.

Faye slipped the reins through her fingers. She grabbed a handful of mane as an anchor. Elan landed and galloped off, taking full advantage of the loose reins, dodging and ducking through the other horses. Faye pulled herself back into position. She fought down the impulse to yank hard on the reins to bring the mare to a sudden halt. Heart thumping, she gently gathered up the slack until she made contact with the bit in Elan's mouth. Instant tension on the other end as the mare braced against the soft pressure. Faye vibrated the reins, clenched and released her fingers, playing the bit like a musical instrument.

The mare yielded. Faye asked for more. Elan gave in to the pressure on her mouth and shifted down to walk.

Faye relaxed her hands. Hot-faced, she turned to Andrew and Mr. Devries.

"A bit slower on the approach next time," called Andrew.

Elan fought against being held back, shaking her head from side to side. Faye darted an anxious glance at the coach. Andrew's arms were crossed, his face unreadable. He said nothing.

Annoyed by the tight restraint of the reins, Elan paid no attention to the jump ahead. The mare couldn't jump like this, fussed and tense, Faye realized. She eased off, prepared for the sudden rush like a rocket from a launching pad. Elan put in an extravagant leap. Faye stayed with her, playing the reins on the far side until the mare was under control again.

Andrew raised the jump.

There was no time to think or ride to a strategy on Elan. All of Faye's senses were on hyper-alert, involved in staying with the mare, keeping up with her lightning-quick acceleration, balancing on top of her flying leaps into the air. She had to trust in her own body's reflexes, in all her years of training and practice. It was the most exhilarating riding she'd ever experienced...and the scariest.

The jump went higher and wider. The crowd in the ring thinned, riders going off to compete in their classes. Andrew put up the other warm-up fences, creating a small course just for Faye and Elan.

And then, coming around a turn to a jump, Faye found she could judge the strides to the takeoff. Elan kept a constant rhythm all the way, lifting off and curling her body over the fence. They touched down and cantered away. Suddenly, it was easy.

Andrew clapped his hands together in the air. "Bravo, Faye! You've got it!"

Faye pushed his words to one side in her head. The next jump was approaching.

The jumps were big; she knew that from the long time they spent in the air over them. Elan arched over them effortlessly, as if the natural law of gravity somehow didn't apply to her. Never in all her years of riding had Faye felt anything like this. There was nothing this mare couldn't soar over, no jump too high or too wide.

They cleared the last pole. Faye eased the mare to walk. She stroked the ebony neck, murmured praise into the slender ears.

"Faye, would you come here, please?" called Andrew.

He and Mr. Devries stood side by side as she rode over. An anxious scan of their faces told her nothing.

"Well done," said Mr. Devries. "You have good hands."

"Thank you...sir."

"Yes, very nice riding, Faye. Now, we've got something to ask you. Would you ride Elan in her class this afternoon?" said Andrew.

Faye blinked at him. Had she heard correctly? "You want me to ride Elan this afternoon? In the horse show?"

"Yes, in the show," he repeated patiently. "I know this is sudden but I have every confidence in your ability."

"I'll do it!"

Andrew beamed. "Laurence, you have a rider."

"Good, good." Mr. Devries reached for and shook Faye's hand. "Thank you very much. She's a wonderful horse, bold and careful, just like her mother."

"Her dam was a grand prix jumper, Faye," said Andrew, "*and* her sire."

"Yes, I bred her to be a top-level show jumper," said the owner. "But she's a twin and didn't grow very tall."

"What happened to the other foal?"

"He's a good-looking horse, big and strong. But he doesn't have Elan's heart." The old man tapped his chest. "And heart is what makes a winner."

Faye nodded, thinking of Robin. "What class is Elan entered in?"

"The Junior derby," said Mr. Devries. He noticed Faye's quick frown. "Is there a problem? Don't tell me you've never ridden a derby class."

Andrew shook his head. "Faye's been in lots of derbies; I've watched her and she's good. *Is* there a problem, Faye?"

"Oh, no," she said hastily, in case Mr. Devries took back his offer. "No problem at all."

"Okay, then. Good thing you've already walked the course. I'm off to the show office to make the arrangements for the change of rider. Laurence, I'll need you to come with me. I'll see you back at the barn, Faye."

"I'm looking forward to watching you jump Elan," said Mr. Devries to Faye. "She'll win if you do a good job."

"I will, sir. I'll ride my very best. I promise."

"I'll hold you to that." He gave Elan another pat and left to join Andrew.

An hour later Faye sat on a bale of hay outside Elan's stall, the mare's bridle draped over her lap, marvelling at the sudden change in her fortune. She rubbed a barely damp sponge moistened with leather cleaner into the straps of the bridle. Over and over in her brain the memory of her incredible ride on Elan played like video footage on continuous loop. She recalled the surge off the ground, the long soaring arc through the air to a landing as soft as falling into a featherbed.

"Faye! Is it true? Are you riding Elan in the Junior derby?"

She looked up to see Nicole standing over her, pale hair askew. Faye nodded.

"But I wouldn't have…" Nicole collapsed onto the bale beside her. "I didn't know she was entered in the derby!"

"Don't worry, Nicole. I can ride *both* of them." Faye had given the situation a great deal of thought. "It will actually work out better this way because I'll have a reason for being in my show clothes. I'll ride Robin or Elan—whoever goes first—then we'll make the switch beside the bleachers, just as we planned. Unless you want to ride Robin yourself?"

"No, I can't do that!"

"Okay, no problem. I'll ride them both." Most professional riders had more than one mount in the big classes, Faye reflected. She was on her way.

"You think I'm a real wimp for not riding in the show,

don't you?" sighed Nicole.

"No," said Faye with a shrug. Dreams of riding Robin—and now Elan—over the derby course filled her brain nearly to overflow. There was very little room for thoughts about anything or anyone else.

"Yes, you do. I know you do. But how could you understand? It's always so easy for you."

It took Faye several moments to tune in. "Huh? What are you talking about?"

"Forget about it," muttered Nicole, getting to her feet.

"I don't understand…hey, where are you going?"

Nicole marched off down the shedrow and turned the corner without a backward glance.

Faye puzzled over Nicole's odd behaviour for a few seconds before returning to her bridle polishing and dreams of glory.

15

Faye prepared to ride. Left leg into her show breeches, then right. Arms into the long sleeves of a pale green riding blouse. Fasten all the little buttons with clumsy fingers.

"Need help?" asked Kirsty as Faye struggled to button the high-necked collar.

"Hmm." Faye lifted her chin.

Nimbly, Kirsty slid the buttons through their tiny openings. "You're very quiet, Faye. Are you nervous?"

Faye blew out a long breath. "A bit. Maybe a lot."

Nicole burst through the curtain. "I just checked the order of go. Elan's in tenth and Robin's thirteenth."

"Only two rides in between," said Faye in dismay.

"That's not much time to—" Nicole broke off, noticing Kirsty. "I'd better get changed." She flung open the lid of her trunk, rifling through the contents.

In front of the tiny mirror tied to the wall with baling twine, Faye studied her reflection. Her black velvet helmet sat low on her head, covering all of her springy red hair except for two narrow bands over her temples—the trademarks that identified her as Faye March. For once she had a reason to be grateful for the bright colour of her hair. She scraped the hair up under the rim of her helmet and became instantly anonymous. Without her hair showing and with sunglasses covering her eyes she could be anyone, even Nicole Walsh.

She pulled her hair back out of her helmet. Since Elan was her first ride she could be herself for now.

"Here's your jacket." Kirsty held out Faye's dark blue riding coat.

"Oh, you must be tired of that old thing. Borrow one of mine," said Nicole hastily. She thrust a grey jacket at Faye.

Faye shrugged it on.

"That jacket is too tight on you," said Kirsty.

"No, it's not," said Nicole. "It looks good."

Faye squeezed into her boots and gathered up her gloves. She waited as Nicole tied back her pale blonde hair and tucked it under her black helmet. She slid on her grey jacket and fastened the buttons, patting the pocket to make sure the sunglasses were still there.

"You two look like...twins," said Kirsty.

Nicole shot Faye a triumphant look. "Really? Come on, sis, time to go ride." She hooked her elbow through Faye's and pulled her out of the tack room. As they walked over to the ring Nicole pulled the sunglasses out and slipped them on.

Mr. Devries held Elan outside the warm-up ring. Glossy purple highlights rippled across the mare's ebony coat as she danced on the spot with impatience. She craned her neck, her bright, dark-eyed gaze zeroing in on her new rider.

"Hey there, pretty mare." Faye ran her gloved hand down the muscled neck. Elan stood still under her touch.

"I have to tighten her girth," said Mr. Devries.

Faye stepped back to give him room and felt a gentle shove between her shoulders. She looked back. "Robin!"

He bunted her again with his head and stamped a front hoof. Then Nicole swung into his saddle and rode into the ring.

"Oh, look at that cute little bay pony," gushed a woman at ringside. "Isn't he sweet?" She pointed at Robin.

Sweet? Faye wrinkled her nose in distaste. Robin was a highly trained athlete, not an overgrown puppy.

"Ready, Faye?" asked Mr. Devries. At her nod he boosted her into Elan's saddle, then reached up and for-mally shook her hand. "Good luck."

Elan knew it was showtime.

She was wildly excited, barely able to contain herself. If Faye let her go she shot into a gallop, tearing around the ring like a racehorse. She tensed every muscle in her neck and shoulders against the restraint of the bit, until Faye's arms and shoulders ached with the strain. Still Elan refused to walk or even trot. Neck bowed until her chin was nearly touching her chest, she cantered on the spot. There was nothing Faye could do to settle the horse down.

"Let's get her over a few fences," called Andrew. "Maybe that will help her focus."

Faye nodded grimly. If she couldn't control Elan in the confines of the warm-up ring, how was she going to manage her out on the course? Her heart crashed against her chest wall as she saw herself clinging for life to the saddle of the black mare while she bolted across the jump field.

"Faye!" Andrew said sharply. He gestured to the jump beside him.

Licking her dry lips, Faye aimed a prancing Elan at the jump.

Elan showed her disdain for the low obstacle by charging over it at top speed. Andrew raised the pole each time but Elan refused to slow down. She flung her head from side to side as Faye pulled her up.

"I don't think I can do this," she chattered, her jaw quaking.

Andrew looked up at her. "Okay, she's tough to ride right now, but when you get her on the course, all by herself, she'll be a different horse. Believe me, Faye, you *can* ride this horse and ride her well."

"But I feel really nervous," she whispered.

"Nerves are part of the game," said Andrew. "We all get nervous. That's how we stay sharp. The thing is, you have to find some way to manage your nerves. Nicole used to have a real problem controlling her nervousness but you can see she's over that now."

They both looked over at Nicole, lolling in Robin's

saddle while she chatted with her parents.

"Ask her what she did. Maybe she can help," suggested the coach.

She got me to ride her pony, that's what, thought Faye. Elan stirred restlessly under her. The black mare was just too much for her—too high-strung, too agile, too powerful. Faye knew she wasn't going to be able to manage to get her around the jump course without a disaster. The best thing would be to scratch out of the class right now before anything went wrong and she embarrassed herself in front of the whole crowd.

She opened her mouth to tell Andrew just that but the coach had moved away to talk to another student.

"She's a lot of horse, isn't she?" Mr. Devries stood at the mare's head, stroking her face.

"Yes, she is," agreed Faye.

"She gets very excited before she competes, but on course she's all business."

This was the time to tell him she wouldn't be riding Elan on course. Faye swallowed to wet her mouth.

"Faye, I like the way you ride my horse. I've got other horses I need ridden in competitions. All of them are good jumpers—though Elan is probably the best. I'm thinking about having you ride them for me…if you win with Elan today."

"Are you serious?" croaked Faye.

The old man frowned. "I sure am. You strike me as a pretty ambitious young rider. I bet you'd like to ride at Spruce Meadows, wouldn't you?"

"Oh, yes!"

"Then that is what we will do," he smiled, "if you win today. Ride your best, Faye." He gave Elan a final pat and moved away.

"Faye, try that fence one more time," called Andrew.

Head spinning, Faye rode toward the jump on automatic pilot. Elan sailed over and loped away.

"Excellent, Faye! You're ready to go!"

The whipper-in called Elan's number. It was their turn.

"Good luck, Faye," shouted Kirsty from ringside.

Faye gathered her reins and asked Elan to canter. To her enormous relief the mare was content to roll along in a steady, relaxed rhythm. They circled, waiting for the judge to give the signal to start. Faye tried to quickly run through the course again but her head was crammed full of images of herself on Elan jumping at Spruce Meadows, flying over enormous jumps, accepting ribbons and trophies. She had to win today. Her whole future depended on it.

At last the buzzer sounded. "Ready, girl?" she whispered to the mare. A thin black ear flicked back to her. She turned Elan to the first jump.

Throw your heart over the fence and the rest will follow. The old adage rose from deep in Faye's memory. Lucy used to say those words to her when she first started riding over fences.

Elan's slender ears snapped forward as she zoned in on the oxer looming in their path. Suddenly they were chasing over the grass, Elan shaking her head violently at Faye's effort to slow her down. They were going too fast and there was nothing Faye could do to check the mare's speed. Her joints and muscles froze with fear. Her hands locked on the reins.

Wrenching the reins free, Elan flew the jump like a steeplechaser, leaving out an entire stride on the take-off side. Faye flopped onto her neck. Pushing herself up she seized back on the reins. The mare threw her head up, mouth gaping to escape the pressure on the bit. Her stride stalled and she fell into trot.

Faye's heart was pounding, chasing the fear through her body like a fever. Precious seconds ticked away as they took a wobbling path to the second jump.

Get going! She clamped her legs against Elan. The mare shot forward, rocketed over the panels and landed in full gallop, charging up the slope to the triple bar.

She closed her eyes as Elan stood far off the base of the huge jump and launched herself. *Please, please, please, let us make it,* she prayed as they flew through the air.

She panted in relief when they safely landed. Tentatively she took back the reins. Elan braced her jaw. "Easy, mare, steady, steady," she chanted, playing the reins like a musician. There was no measurable response from the runaway mare.

Another spasm of fear quaked through her. The most challenging parts of the course lay ahead. She had to get back into command. She could feel her throat going dry, her muscles stiffening. What if Elan misjudged and crashed right through a jump? What if she slipped and fell galloping around a turn? Faye could feel them slamming to the ground, her limbs pinned under a thousand pounds of panicked horse.

Stop! Mentally, she grabbed those thoughts and pushed them out of her head. She had to fill her brain with something, anything, to keep them from creeping back in.

She began to sing. "Row, row, row your boat!"

Elan's ear twitched at the sound of her voice.

"Gently down the stream," puffed Faye. She wasn't just imagining it: Elan's stride was steadier, matching the rhythm of the song. "Merrily, merrily, merrily, merrily, life is but a dream," and they were up and over the triple bar and bouncing on.

The stone wall loomed. Did they have a chance of making the tight inside turn? There was no other choice. Faye suddenly realized she hadn't walked the outside track, didn't know exactly where to turn. They had to go inside.

Faye fixed her eyes on the spot past the stone wall where they'd have to land to make the inside turn. Elan pulled against her hands, eager to jump. Abruptly she tore the reins through Faye's fingers and charged the wall.

"Whoa," Faye screeched uselessly as Elan touched down and barrelled on. There was no time to make the turn. They were among the maze of jumps, dodging and ducking, trying to find a clear path. Over top of the tall white standards she saw the liverpool. Eyes glued to the jump she sent Elan at it, trusting her to somehow make her way through. The mare twisted her agile frame between the other jumps, her nimble hooves skipping over and around the bases of the standards. Faye's foot knocked against a solid wood upright. Pain hammered through her and she gasped in shock. Before she could help herself she glanced down.

Elan burst into the open. Quickly Faye looked up again. The liverpool was right in front, only three strides away. No time to do anything but ride forward at the jump. She closed her legs.

The mare's neck came up as she took in the wide expanse of water at the bottom of the jump. Her hesitation flowed into Faye like an electric current.

Resolutely, Faye pitched her heart over the jump. She followed it with her eyes, imagining the place where it landed. Growling deep in her throat she clamped her legs into Elan's girth. "Go!"

Elan exploded into the air. The arc of her leap carried them high above the liverpool, so high it seemed the mare would never return to earth. Like an arrow she floated through space with Faye tucked tight into her saddle. Her head dipped, her front knees unfolded as they began their descent.

As softly as a bird Elan landed and galloped on. Faye pointed her toward the next jump. They were together now, trust in each other growing stride by stride. Jump after jump passed beneath them until finally there were no more. With a whoop, Faye released the reins and Elan swept through the finish.

Faye steadied her to a strutting walk. Suddenly she was trembling all over, tears blurring her vision.

"That was awesome! I've never seen you ride like that!" Kirsty caught hold of Elan's reins as they came out the gate.

"Wonderful riding, Faye," said Andrew. "Absolutely terrific!"

Mr. Devries patted Elan's neck over and over. "Very good!"

People crowded around praising and congratulating the horse and Faye. She kicked her feet free and slid down onto wobbly legs. "I have to go." She hurried away.

Kirsty passed the mare to Mr. Devries and ran after her. "Faye, are you okay?"

Faye crumpled onto a patch of grass behind the bleachers. She shook her head. "I was so scared."

"You were?" Kirsty knelt beside her. She wrapped her arm around her friend's shoulders. "But you rode so well. Everyone said so."

"It was all Elan. I was just along for the ride."

"Faye, what are you doing sitting here?" Nicole scurried over and tugged her to her feet. "Come on!"

Faye had completely forgotten about riding Robin. Nicole towed her to the end of the bleachers where the bay stood patiently waiting, his reins looped over the metal supports.

"Take off your helmet," said Nicole.

"Ouch," protested Faye as Nicole's fingers raked her sweat-dampened hair off her temples. The other girl yanked the helmet from her grasp and slid it carefully onto her head. Faye winced as Nicole poked the few remaining stray hairs under the brim.

Nicole dug the sunglasses out of her pocket and hooked the arms over Faye's ears. "Okay, you're good. Let's go."

She led Robin around the end of the bleachers so he was out of sight of Andrew's group while Faye mounted. She gathered the reins, surprised to find herself so near the ground. When had he become so small?

"Hurry," urged Nicole. "It's nearly your turn."

Faye scooted Robin around the bleachers and pulled him up. Kirsty blocked the way. "What are you doing?"

Faye looked helplessly down at Nicole, who shuffled Kirsty aside so Robin could pass. "Please, please, don't say anything," Nicole begged.

Kirsty looked over Nicole's shoulder at Faye. "Why are you doing this?"

"Just this once. To help Nicole," said Faye.

"But how is this helping—"

"Nicole! Get over here," called Andrew. "They're holding the gate for you."

"Go!" hissed Nicole, ducking behind the bleachers.

Faye dug her heels into Robin, hustling him into the ring. The buzzer sounded and the pony bounded into canter. She sent him to the first fence.

Framed between the tiny, curved ears, the oxer loomed

as large as a house. Faye hugged her legs against Robin and trusted the pony to find the best takeoff spot. He skipped up to the base of the huge jump and sprang up like a grasshopper. Faye reached forward with her arms to free up the reins, her fingertips nearly reaching the top of his neck.

They touched down and scampered on. A grin pulled at Faye's cheeks as Robin bounced up and over jump after jump. Teaming up with her trusted old partner was like coming home.

At fence four Robin knew exactly what she wanted. He shortened his stride coming in, hopped over the wall, then wheeled to the left. Faye urged him on. He flattened out and galloped at the liverpool. She squeezed tight with her legs. For an instant the pony hesitated. Then he bravely flung himself over the water jump.

Even as they hung in the air Faye realized her mistake. Robin was no Elan with a powerful jump that could clear the moon. She'd asked him to take off from too far away. There was no way his compact body could stretch out enough to clear the height and breadth of the fence. She waited to hear the clunk of the top rail hitting the ground.

Robin seemed to buck in mid-air, kicking his heels up. The rail rattled in the jump cups, then...silence. As they came down Faye risked a quick glance back. The top rail of the liverpool sat securely in its cups.

"Thank you, Robbie," she whispered, her gratitude forming a lump in her throat. There'd never been a pony as brave and clever as this one. There never would be.

After that she remembered to leave him alone and let him jump the fences his way.

The last fence came all too soon. The pony hopped over and dashed through the finish. Faye slowed him down to walk. Their round together had been so easy she was barely puffing. A gentle wave of sadness wafted over her. Her final ride on Robin was over. To a smattering of applause they left the ring.

Nicole and Kirsty waited at the far end of the bleachers. Marching along on a long rein Robin lifted his head and nickered. Nicole ran up and threw her arms around his neck. "Oh, Robin, you were fantastic!"

"Quick, get down! Here come her parents," Kirsty told Faye.

She slid off Robin just as Mr. and Mrs. Walsh rounded the corner of the bleachers. Andrew was right behind.

"Oh, darling, that was wonderful!" Irene Walsh hugged Nicole.

"Excellent riding, sweetheart, just excellent." Her father patted her back. "It looks like you've got that pony straightened right out. Now, just go all out in the jump-off and first place will be yours."

"Good round, Nicole," said Andrew. "Your week at Hillcroft Farm obviously paid off." He lifted his eyebrows at Faye, standing off to one side with Kirsty.

He knows, thought Faye. She shifted under the coach's sharp gaze.

"How many are in the jump-off?" asked Nicole.

"Just three so far—you, the rider on that fat grey and Faye. But there are still quite a few first rounds to go," said her father.

The jump-off, thought Faye. *I have to ride Elan...but Nicole...Robin...*

"Faye? Are you all right?" asked Andrew.

He caught her shoulders and guided her to the lowest bench in the bleachers.

"I feel funny," she said after sitting down.

Mrs. Walsh pulled off her helmet and the blonde hairnet. "You look pale, hon. Did you eat lunch? I didn't think so," she said as Faye shook her head. She dug in her tiny knapsack and came up with a chocolate bar. "This will give you energy. I always keep a few with me for Nicole. She has problems eating when she's nervous, too."

She ripped open the wrapping of the chocolate bar and handed it to Faye.

"But I'm not..." It wasn't true, Faye realized. She *was* nervous. Really nervous. Her arms and legs were trembling while her head was floating somewhere above the rest of her body. She couldn't ride—not Elan, not Robin—while she felt like this. "I feel sick. I don't think I can ride."

"Kirsty, would you get Faye a bottle of water? And Ken, would you check in with the other kids? Tell them I'll be there soon," said Andrew. He sat down on the bench. "What's going on?"

"I don't feel good. It must be the flu."

"Hmm. Have a bite of that chocolate bar. You need to eat something."

Reluctantly Faye swallowed a bite of chocolate, sending it down into her churning stomach. To her surprise it stayed there. She ate another piece.

"You know, Faye, nerves are tricky. You need them to keep you keen but if they get out of hand they can shut you right down."

"But I'm not scared," Faye insisted. "I love jumping."

"I know you do, Faye. But being scared isn't the only reason a person gets nervous. Sometimes it's because an athlete wants to do her very best. Especially if there's a lot on the line."

Faye felt stronger, her head anchored back onto her neck. Again she wondered if Nicole's coach knew what she and Nicole had been up to, if he knew just how much was on the line.

"Everything happens so fast with Elan!" she said at last. "What if I make a mistake? She'll knock a rail or run out. I could even fall off. Then I'll lose the class and Mr. Devries won't let me ride for him anymore—"

"Whoa right there! Let me ask you a question. What if you scratch? How will you feel then?"

Just the thought of not having to ride Elan in a jump-off against the clock filled Faye with relief. "Better. My stomach won't hurt." *And there's always Robin*, she added silently.

"And later on, when the derby is done and the awards are being handed out: how will you feel then?"

For the first time, Faye pictured herself standing on the sidelines, watching while Nicole collected the ribbons she and Robin had earned. "I...I don't know."

Andrew fell silent. He leaned forward, elbows on knees, intent on the horse and rider in the ring.

"I've never ridden a horse like Elan," Faye said.

The coach nodded and said nothing.

"She's so powerful and fast. I can hardly control her. But..." Faye bit her lip, remembering those racehorse sprints and soaring leaps. She'd never felt anything like that before...and might never again, if she scratched now. Yet how could she bear the thought of losing Robin forever?

In the ring the rider had finished his round. "Eight faults," said Andrew, sitting up. "You know, Faye, it's not surprising that you feel on edge right now." He looked her right in the eye. "This isn't what you expected, is it?"

Faye looked straight back at him. They both knew what they were talking about, now. "So what do I do?"

"Depends what you've got in here, Faye." Andrew tapped his chest. "Look deep in your heart. Then you'll know."

The coach swung down off the bench. "Now, I'd better check on Nicole. Something tells me I should send her over a few practice fences before she goes into the jump-off."

Faye remained sitting in the bleachers, staring with unseeing eyes at the competitors jumping around the course.

Five minutes ticked slowly past. Like water filling a bucket, certainty flowed into her. She *knew* what she was going to do. And she knew how she was going to do it.

"And that was the final competitor in the first round of our Junior derby," boomed the announcer over the loudspeaker. "Tough course, folks: only three riders will be coming back to compete in the jump-off. There'll be a short break while the jump crew gets the course ready."

Faye swung off the bench. It was time for a talk with Nicole. She had something to tell her.

16

"You promised!" screeched Nicole. "You have to ride him!"

"Shhh! Do you want someone to hear?" Faye glanced around but no one seemed to be paying them any attention. Just the same, she pitched her voice low. "I can't ride both Elan and Robin in the jump-off. With only three horses competing there won't be time for me to switch."

"Scratch Elan! Say she feels lame or…say you're sick! That's it; you've got food poisoning. Tell them that and then you can hide in the toilet until it's time for you to ride Robin."

"No, I'm not going to do that. I'm going to ride Elan and you're going to ride Robin."

"I can't!"

"Yes, you can! Now listen carefully because I'm going to tell you how. Do you understand what I'm saying?"

Nicole's eyes widened. "You're going to give me the secret."

"Yes," agreed Faye solemnly. "It's time for you to know."

"Nicole, honey, it's time! Bring your pony over here,"

called Irene Walsh.

"Mom, not right now!"

"Come on, sweetheart, Andrew's waiting for you to take a practice jump. You can chat with Faye later."

"I'll be there in a moment! Faye, tell me quick."

"Okay, the course is set and we're ready for our first competitor in the jump-off," said the announcer.

The stocky grey trotted into the ring to enthusiastic applause to begin his jump-off. The judge sounded the buzzer to signal the start of the round.

"Hurry! I'm in next. I have to know!"

"Sing to him," Faye said. "That's the secret."

"*Sing?* That's all I have to do? Just...sing?"

"Yes, all the way around the course."

"Okay, I can do that. I've had lots of singing lessons. So what should I sing?"

"Try 'Row, Row, Row Your Boat.' You know that song, don't you?"

"Of course. You're sure this will work?"

"Yes," said Faye with as much confidence as she could put into a single word. Hadn't it worked with Elan? Singing had filled her head, blocked out panic and unthawed her frozen arms and legs. The simple rhythm had joined her and her horse like a pair of dancers.

The grey trundled to the first jump in the modified course. Fences one to five were the same as the first round, but then the course changed, leaving out jumps and adding several new ones to create a twisting track that called for tight riding and bold jumping to make a fast time. The grey's tail was swishing, his rider's mouth set in a grim line. A gasp rose from the spectators as the horse slid to a stop in front of the oxer. His rider circled him and sent him at the jump again. This time he popped over to a chorus of cheers.

"He's going to have a slow time," said Nicole, nodding her chin at the rider on the grey.

"And penalties for that refusal."

"Looks like it's between you and me now. You know I *have* to win, don't you, Faye?"

"I know." Faye shrugged. "I've told you the secret. That's all I can do."

"Maybe you could not try so hard to win," said Nicole hesitantly. "Maybe you could just go a bit slow or take all the outside turns. After all, you've only ridden Elan once. No one would blame you for it."

Not long ago Faye had been searching for excuses not to ride the volatile black mare in the jump-off. Now she not only wanted to do it, she wanted to win. And she knew exactly what Nicole was asking her to do.

Nicole saw her hesitation. "Come on, Faye, you're a good rider. There'll be another Elan for you. But this is it for me and Robin. I know you're not crazy about me— but do it for him. Do it for Robin."

Swallowing hard, Faye nodded. "I'll let you win."

"Oh, Faye, thank you so much." Nicole stretched out her arms and threw them around Faye in a quick hug. "You're the best friend in the whole world."

"Nicole, why aren't you on that pony?" demanded

Andrew. "Get up, you're in next!"

"I'm coming!" Grinning, Nicole swung aboard Robin and charged off to the practice jumps.

The jump crew dashed into the ring as the grey horse jigged out the gate, his rider scowling fiercely.

"Nicole Walsh, you're in!" shouted the whipper-in.

"Here we are!" Nicole and Robin galloped past the defeated grey onto the grass field.

The buzzer went. The round had begun.

Faye's chest felt tight from her swollen heart as Robin cantered at the first jump, dark eyes bright. He lifted his knees and skipped over. Nicole folded tight to the saddle, her arms stretching forward. As they rolled on to the second fence Faye saw her lips moving.

Kirsty jogged over to stand beside Elan. "What's that noise Nicole's making?"

"She's singing."

"Singing?" Robin bounced up to the wall, jumped at an angle and made the inside turn. "Look at her go!"

Andrew appeared. "Brilliant idea, Faye! Absolutely brilliant. Singing! I should have thought of that long ago."

"Come on, Nicole, that's my girl!" Ken Walsh was on his feet in the bleachers.

Robin flew the last fence and beetled through the timers.

"She's clear!" Andrew clasped his hands to the sky. "Hallelujah! Thank you, Faye. You are a real sportsman."

"Sportswoman," corrected Kirsty.

Faye saw only Robin, bright-eyed, snorting with pride,

high-stepping over the shining green grass. Nicole threw her arms around his arched neck and hugged him.

"Isn't he the best pony in the whole world?" she demanded, coming out the gate. "I hardly touched the reins. He did it all; it was as though he knew what I was thinking."

"Darling, that was fantastic!" cried Irene Walsh.

"Good job, Nicole," said her father. "Very, very good." He gave Robin a hearty pat. "Looks like you're coming around, old son."

"See, I told you he was, Daddy."

"Well, he hasn't won the class yet. Faye still has her round."

The whipper-in called Faye's number.

She felt a flicker of panic. She'd nearly forgotten about her jump-off round. She dug her heels into Elan.

"Whoa, there," said Andrew, catching the black mare's bridle. "No need to rush."

Faye took a deep breath and struggled to compose herself.

"How are you, my lovely Elan?" Mr. Devries stroked the mare's neck. He looked up. "And how is my rider? All set?"

"I think so."

The bushy eyebrows knitted together. "You think? You don't know? Remember what I said before, Faye. I am a fair man but I expect results from my rider." Giving Elan another pat he returned to his seat.

"This could be a real opportunity for you, Faye," said

Andrew. "Now take it. Ride like you've never ridden before. Good luck!"

And she was in the ring on a goose-stepping Elan, her heart thumping and adrenalin spurting through her veins. The mare felt like a rocket beneath her—one wrong signal and she would launch them both into outer space.

She couldn't do it. Her brain went cloudy; she couldn't think what she was supposed to do next. Her limbs tightened against the horse, muscles seizing up. She was breathing quickly, too quickly, in short gasps, but she couldn't seem to expand her lungs to get in a full breath.

The judge pressed the buzzer. Elan plunged into canter—had she asked her? They flew over the grass while Faye tried to recall the location of the first fence. Racing toward the end of the ring they turned...and there it was. Elan's slender ears framed the wide oxer. She surged toward the jump.

They were airborne, soaring forever over the oxer. Faye grabbed a hank of mane and tucked into the saddle, her body responding to years of practice. They were down and galloping on, Elan sighting the second fence. She flew it like a steeplechaser.

The wind of their passing screeched in Faye's ears. Elan braced her neck as Faye took back the reins, trying to slow the headlong pace as they swooped up the slope to the triple bar. No time to place the mare to the fence; Elan found her own takeoff, catapulting over the widely spaced rails as if they were sticks on the ground.

At the peak of their ascent Faye was sure she could touch heaven.

The stone wall next. Faye tightened her hold even more, desperately trying to shorten Elan's stride to make the turn after. The mare shook her head, locking her jaw against the bit. Faye pulled hard, abandoning tact and finesse. The mare grabbed the bit and bolted, launching herself at the wall a full stride out. Faye folded her body close to the horse's arching frame. Wind-tears blurred her eyes but she didn't need to see to know they were flying higher than she'd ever been before. But there was no time for shock or surprise. Elan landed and charged on.

They'd missed the inside turn completely. The chance to shave valuable seconds off their time was lost. There was no hope of winning now. Unless…

Faye blinked rapidly, clearing her vision. She slammed her heels into the mare's sides. "Go!" she shrieked. "Go, go, go!"

Elan shot forward like a bullet. They pounded around the far turn, chunks of turf flying up from the mare's hooves. Hunkered down against the withers, Faye prayed Elan wouldn't slip. One hoof sliding and they'd fall together—

She snatched up that thought and shut it out of her head. The liverpool was in front of them. A shaft of sunlight broke through the clouds and sparkled on the water in the trough below.

Steady back or move up? For a fateful moment, Faye dithered, trying to pick the best approach.

Elan didn't hesitate. She lifted over the flimsy top rail and galloped on.

Faye laughed, delighting in the mare's bravery. There was nothing this glorious horse wouldn't—or couldn't—jump. Up and down the banks, over the ditches, through the combination, Elan jumped every obstacle with delightful ease.

The last two fences were like cavaletti. Bounce, bounce and they were over, the timers directly ahead in their path. As they swept through, Faye felt a fleeting jab of disappointment. Was it over already?

Whooping with joy, she galloped Elan around the entire ring before easing her up. Kirsty and Andrew ran up to them as they pranced to the gate.

"You're crazy, do you know that?" shrieked Kirsty. "She looked like a racehorse, she went so fast."

Andrew caught the mare's reins. Faye kicked her feet free of the stirrups and vaulted out of the saddle. She loosened the mare's girth. Stepping up to the mare's head she looked into the deep, dark eyes. "Thank you," she whispered.

Elan bowed her head and pressed it against Faye. She reached up and fondled a slim black ear.

"Well done, Faye," said Andrew softly.

"Thanks," she said thickly.

Laurence Devries grasped her hand and shook it vigorously. "Good, good, very good." He let go and patted his mare's neck, murmuring praise.

Faye was surrounded by praise and congratulations.

"You took three seconds off Nicole's time, do you know that?" said Kirsty. "You won!"

"We did? That's—" And then she was hit with a jolt of shock. She'd completely forgotten her promise to let Nicole and Robin win. She looked up and saw Nicole, still mounted on Robin, staring at her with huge, grey eyes.

Elan bunted her again, still thoroughly excited by their thrilling round together.

"Yes, you should be proud," Mr. Devries said to the mare. "You are wonderful." He hugged Faye's shoulders. "Thank you again. You've made me very happy. I'm going to talk to your grandmother about having you ride my other jumpers. What do you think of that?"

"That would be great!" said Faye. But her smile faded as soon as she turned her face back to the Walshes.

Mr. Walsh had pulled Andrew aside.

"Daddy, please, no!" Nicole slid from the pony. "You saw: we jumped clear."

"Sweetie, he isn't fast enough. You won't win in the jump-offs."

Faye felt a chill. Ken Walsh was really going to do it. He was going to sell Robin far away to California. She would never see him again—and Nicole…

Nicole's voice was raised now. "Daddy, if you sell Robin I'll stop riding!"

Looking around at the curious heads turned toward them, Mr. Walsh chuckled uncomfortably. "Honey, you don't mean that," he said.

"Oh yes I do. I'll quit. I'll never get on another pony ever again."

"But, Nicole, think of all the years of work you've put in," said Irene. "You would be wasting your talent."

"Come on, be sensible, the pony just isn't good enough for you," stated Ken Walsh.

"Daddy, you just don't get it. You don't understand *anything*. Robin and I are partners! We know each other now and the more we work together the better we'll get. We need more time!"

Her father looked bemused. "Partners, huh?"

"Yes, partners. And know what? I think we did really well together in our rounds. This was Faye's lucky day but next time…" Nicole paused dramatically. "Next time we're going to win!"

Ken Walsh slung an arm over his daughter's shoulders. "That's my girl. All right, keep the pony. I guess every partnership needs time to grow."

Faye sighed with relief.

"Oh, Dad, Mom, you're the best!" Nicole hugged her father and mother and then Robin.

"She *always* gets her own way," Kirsty whispered to Faye.

Not always, Faye thought. For only minutes later she was lined up in the ring on Elan, her heart singing with the joy of her triumph as the lower placings were announced.

And then she heard the announcer saying, "…proud to present the first-place ribbon and trophy to Elan, owned by Mr. Laurence Devries and ridden to victory by Faye March!"

Applause burst over them like a summer shower. Proudly arching her neck, Elan danced on the spot. Faye's cheeks stretched wide in a smile she was sure she would wear forever.

Mr. Devries led Elan out of the lineup to the waiting photographer. Positioning himself at the mare's head, Mr. Devries cradled the trophy in his arms, beaming a grin as large as Faye's up at her.

The photographer crouched down. "Okay, big smiles from the winners!"

When the photographer had taken several shots Kirsty ran up to Elan. She held up Andrew's cell phone to Faye. "Someone wants to speak to you."

"Who is it?"

Kirsty waggled her eyebrows and grinned.

"Hello?"

"Faye," said a husky voice.

"Lucy, is that you? Are you okay?"

"I'm just fine." Silence. "Girl, I'm so proud of you. So's Riley. For winning…and everything else."

Faye tried to swallow away the lump in her throat.

"Sure wish I could've been there to see you." Her grandmother paused, inhaled a breath. "I love you."

She couldn't help herself; it was all too much to hold in. Faye burst into tears.

17

Faye slipped into Elan's dark stall. She rested against the wall, utterly spent, soothed by the monotonous crunching of large teeth grinding hay. Warmth radiated from the mare's body through the cooling night air. Faye breathed in the comforting scents of crushed grass and salt and the tang of manure. Comfort wrapped around her like a soft wool blanket.

She heaved a long sigh, echoed by Elan. There was nowhere as peaceful as a stable at night. Her eyes adjusted to the gloom. Andrew's grooms were the best but Lucy's training was hard to put aside. She crouched down, checking the mare's stable bandages to make sure they were on securely and not binding in any place. Elan left her hay net and nuzzled the back of her neck.

"Hey, that tickles." Faye blew softly into the mare's nostrils in a horse-style greeting. "You're amazing, know that? A superhorse."

Elan snorted in agreement and returned to her hay.

For the first time Faye didn't feel the sting of disloyalty to her old partner. Elan *was* a super jumper— brave, careful, agile and scopey. Faye accepted now that

Robin would never jump as fast or as high. He had so much to offer a rider coming up through the ranks—experience, reliability and a heart as big as a house. But still...did that rider have to be Nicole Walsh?

She rocked back on her heels and stood up. "Oh, I'm so full."

Delighted by Elan's win, Mr. Devries had taken everyone in the barn out to a celebration dinner, except the Walshes who had relatives to visit. Now they were doing a late-night barn check before heading back to the hotel. Tomorrow would be a long day of packing up and travelling home.

"Well, I'd better let you get your rest," Faye told the mare. On an impulse she reached around the mare's neck and hugged. Elan started, then relaxed. She stood completely still, even those ever-questing ears for once at rest, until Faye let go. "Night, Elan."

The mare left her hay and trailed her to the stall door. "No, you have to stay here." Faye gently pushed the mare's head back in the stall as she tried to follow her out.

Walking away, Faye looked back over her shoulder. Elan remained at the door, watching her leave with that deep, dark gaze that seemed to look into her very soul.

Robin whinnied as she went past his stall. Faye was at his door and reaching in to pet him before she realized Nicole was inside with him. "Oh, hi." She let her arm fall to her side.

"Hi!" Nicole gave the pony's neck a final pat and squeezed out the door.

Faye was surprised at how friendly Nicole seemed. She'd expected the other girl to be bitter and resentful about losing.

"I was giving Robin a massage. I'll get the massage therapist to work on him when we get home," chattered Nicole.

"Does he have a problem?"

"Oh, no, I just want him to be comfortable. He works so hard. Don't you, Robin? We wouldn't want you to be stiff and sore, would we?"

Robin munched the sugar cube she gave him, bobbing his head for more.

Faye had never fed him sugar cubes, only carrots or apples as a healthier treat.

"He sure loves his treats," said Nicole, slipping the pony another cube. "Hey, congratulations on winning. You rode really well."

"Oh. Thanks," said Faye warily. She hesitated, then dove in. "Aren't you mad at me for not letting you win?"

Nicole shrugged. "I *almost* won. And I will next time, now that I know the secret to getting Robin to perform. So watch out, Faye."

"You think you can beat me and Elan? It won't be easy, you know."

"I'm going to try my hardest. You can't win *all* the time, Faye, not now that I'm riding Robin."

Faye thought of Elan and her incredible soaring leaps into the air and gazelle-swift sprints. A nervous tingle zipped along her spine just remembering how it felt to be teamed up with all that power and speed. With time and practice together they would become familiar with each other. Become partners. Suddenly her head was crowded with images. Scene after scene flashed through her mind: Elan rocketing over huge fences, spinning around jump-off turns, prancing up to accept the winner's trophy under a broad, blue prairie sky at Spruce Meadows.

Faye stared through the dim light at Robin's dear, honest face. His black eyes were bright and shining, the tiny, curved ears cupped toward her. She reached out and smoothed his bushy forelock down his white blaze, feeling the contentment radiating from him.

"I'll take good care of him, Faye," Nicole was saying. "I promise you. The very best, forever and always."

"There you two are." Kirsty swooped in between them, linking elbows. "I've been sent to tell you to hurry up. Everyone's waiting. Come on, it's time to go home."

About the Author

Julie White started making up horse stories at a young age after her parents told her she couldn't keep a pony in the backyard of their Vancouver home. When she was twelve, her family moved onto a farm near Vernon in the interior of British Columbia, and she got her first horse, a headstrong chestnut named Roger.

Julie lives on a horse farm near Armstrong,

Author photo by Diana Inselberg

B.C. Along with her husband, Robert, a former jockey, she raises thoroughbreds for racing and jumping. She rides every day and competes in jumping classes at horse shows, often against her two grown daughters. She's a Pony Club examiner, riding instructor and course designer.

High Fences is Julie's second book, a sequel to the award-winning *The Secret Pony*.

More pony adventures from author Julie White

The Secret Pony

Kirsty's got a secret—a big, four-legged secret . . .

When they moved out to the country after the divorce, Mom promised Kirsty a pony of her own. Unfortunately, money is tighter than they expected. Then Lancelot practically drops in Kirsty's lap, and she empties her money box to buy him. He's skinny and starved and only half trained for riding. But he's hers, all hers, and Kirsty is overwhelmed with joy.

Because of Lancelot, Kirsty finds a new friend, Faye, whose grandmother, Lucy, runs a pony farm. Because of their friendship, she finds a place to board her pony, and because she makes herself so useful around the place, she finds herself signed up for riding lessons as well. But what she can't seem to find are the words to tell her mother that the pony she'll be riding is her own.

☆ *Our Choice Award*
☆ *Chocolate Lily Award*